Don't Be Talkin'

RECITATIONS AND OTHER FOOLISHNESS FROM NEWFOUNDLAND AND LABRADOR

HARRY INGRAM

FLANKER PRESS LIMITED
ST. JOHN'S

Library and Archives Canada Cataloguing in Publication

Title: Don't be talkin' : recitations and other foolishness from Newfoundland and Labrador / Harry Ingram.
Other titles: Do not be talking | Recitations and other foolishness from Newfoundland and Labrador
Names: Ingram, Harry, author.
Description: Humour.
Identifiers: Canadiana (print) 2021017031X | Canadiana (ebook) 20210173513 | ISBN 9781774570289 (softcover) | ISBN 9781774570319 (PDF) | ISBN 9781774570296 (EPUB)
Subjects: LCSH: Canadian wit and humor—Newfoundland and Labrador. | LCSH: Newfoundland and Labrador—Humor. | CSH: Canadian wit and humor (English)—Newfoundland and Labrador.
Classification: LCC PN6178.C3 I54 2021 | DDC C818/.602—dc23

© 2021 by Harry Ingram

ALL RIGHTS RESERVED. No part of the work covered by the copyright hereon may be reproduced or used in any form or by any means—graphic, electronic or mechanical—without the written permission of the publisher. Any request for photocopying, recording, taping, or information storage and retrieval systems of any part of this book shall be directed to Access Copyright, The Canadian Copyright Licensing Agency, 1 Yonge Street, Suite 800, Toronto, ON M5E 1E5. This applies to classroom use as well.

PRINTED IN CANADA

This paper has been certified to meet the environmental and social standards of the Forest Stewardship Council® (FSC®) and comes from responsibly managed forests, and verified recycled sources.

FLANKER PRESS LTD.
PO BOX 2522, STATION C
ST. JOHN'S, NL
CANADA

TELEPHONE: (709) 739-4477   FAX: (709) 739-4420   TOLL-FREE: 1-866-739-4420

WWW.FLANKERPRESS.COM

9 8 7 6 5 4 3 2 1

The publisher acknowledges the financial support of the Government of Canada through the Canada Book Fund (CBF) and the Government of Newfoundland and Labrador, Department of Tourism, Culture, Industry and Innovation for our publishing activities. We acknowledge the support of the Canada Council for the Arts, which last year invested $157 million to bring the arts to Canadians throughout the country. *Nous remercions le Conseil des arts du Canada de son soutien. L'an dernier, le Conseil a investi 157 millions de dollars pour mettre de l'art dans la vie des Canadiennes et des Canadiens de tout le pays.*

This book is dedicated to my two beautiful daughters, Abigail and Cassandra, from whom I've gotten much inspiration for many of the recitations I write. Your love and support is as awesome as you both are.

Contents

ix
Introduction

1
Don't Be Talkin'

7
Good Night Little One

13
A Son-in-Law's Lament

21
Christmas Is Here!

25
Hands of Time

27
Fox in the Henhouse

33
Just inside the Gate

39
Simple Things

43
Hot Sauce

49
The Wedding That Almost Wasn't

53
My Childhood Christmas

55
Helping Hand

59
The Square Root of Pie

63
Mildred and Mose

67
Don't Ask

71
Havoc at the North Pole

79
Three Stones

83
The Fair

89
The Lobster Tale

93
Home to Stay

99
The One about the Pig

103
Great-Uncle John's Christmas

109
Dad's Old Wooden Flat

113
Trouble with Tea Buns

117
Mary's Crowd

123
Winter

127
The Unfinished Story

131
The Remote

133
Up in Smoke

137
Jerome

143
Whatchamabot

147
The Long Road

155
Arson Around

161
Dog Harbour Treasure

167
C Is for Christmas

169
Bert's Not Well

173
Some Assembly Required

177
The Other End of This

181
Acknowledgements

Introduction

Hello, everyone! I'm Harry Ingram, and welcome to my first book, *Don't Be Talkin'*.

All my life my family has been my most important constant. During my younger years I always had a close bond with my parents and siblings, and this has only grown stronger with time. Then as I married and began a family of my own, I realized that family will always be number one. I tried my best to capture this sentiment between the covers of this lighthearted book. I hope this collection of stories and recitations fills you with warm feelings of relaxation, enjoyment, and laughter.

Recitations have always been a core part of my life growing up in Arnold's Cove. I would listen to them on the radio and on a couple of old records we had around the house. Then there was my Uncle Mose, who would write and perform them as well. It wasn't long before I was reciting works from John Joe English, Leo O'Brien, and Baxter Wareham. It was then I knew I was on to something.

It wasn't until my dad passed away nearly ten years ago that I wrote my first short piece, titled "Hands of Time." I kind of liked what I had written and wondered if there was more in me. Who knew that a few short years later I'd be here sharing my words with all of you? Who knew that I would become an author?

What I hope to accomplish with this book is put smiles on faces. I hope it warms your heart and makes your day a little brighter. If you get as much enjoyment from reading this as I have had writing it, I believe I will have reached my goal.

Read, take it in, enjoy!

Harry

This title piece is a fun story of my fictitious Great-Uncle John. Let's face it. We all know someone like it.

Don't Be Talkin'

Everyone knows one,
And that there's no doubt,
Someone all negative,
Yes, down in the mouth.

I know one quite well,
He's my Great-Uncle John,
But it's not of his wit,
Or his charm I'm so fond.

But crooked as sin,
That's a way to describe 'im,
Opinions he got,
And don't care if you like 'em.

Yes, he's that friggin' crooked,
I'll tell you right now,
If he died tomorrow,
He'd be screwed in the ground.

HARRY INGRAM

I visited one day,
He was watching TV,
Leafs and Habs,
Yes, he loves his hockey.

How's the game, Uncle John?
I asked with a smile,
Then I stopped and waited,
To hear his reply.

Hockey! Don't be talkin'!

They should learn how to skate,
That ref should be shot,
And I'm sure that me Leafs,
Won't make the playoffs.

And I can't see the puck,
Unless I'm wearing my glasses,
The TV's too small,
Where's my bread and molasses?

He talked for five minutes,
About hockey and stuff,
'Til Aunt Suze from the kitchen,
Brought out his mug-up.

I s'pose you're all right now,
With your tea and your lunch,
I said to my uncle,
And he started to grunt.

DON'T BE TALKIN'

Grub! Don't be talkin'.

My son, grub around here,
Is not fit to eat,
Sure, a boiler of soup,
Might have nar bit of meat.

And pea soup is worse,
'Cause most times it's salty,
The broth's almost clear,
And the doughballs are soggy.

And Aunt Suze bakes her cakes,
Like the one in the song,
The Trinity cake,
It will paralyze your jaw.

Yes, it's hard to get grub,
That's fit around here,
Sure, Health Sciences would be better,
Or maybe St. Clare's.

Just then the radio,
Gave tomorrow's forecast,
It should be half cold,
And a touch overcast.

Nice day tomorrow, Uncle John,
You agree?
He stood up and looked out,
The window to see.

HARRY INGRAM

Weather! My son, don't be talkin'.

Sure, one day it's raining,
And the next day snow,
And with frost in the ground,
Me taties won't grow.

And the crowd on the radio,
Sure, they're always wrong,
Sure, they couldn't forecast,
Placentia Bay fog.

Yes, the weather is miserable,
It's never no good,
Sure, I can hardly get out,
To cleave up me wood.

And I can't check me slips,
'Cause 'tis wet and 'tis cold,
I can't even hunt moose,
They says I'm too old.

So I'll stay in the house,
'Til the weather comes fine,
I s'pose I'll get out,
Again 'fore I dies.

Sure you will, Uncle John,
You're still pretty spry,
How ya feelin' these days?
You look the best kind.

DON'T BE TALKIN'

How am I feelin'? Don't be talkin'!

The gout is some bad,
And I got corns on me feet,
And I can't say the last time,
I had a good sleep.

And the piles is right bad,
Not to mention arthritis,
I'm sure I got TB,
Or chronic bronchitis.

Me hearing's not well,
No more is me sight,
And me pants are all shrinking,
I think I might need to diet.

He continued on,
With more aches and more pains,
The ailments would send,
Normal men to their graves.

Well, 'tis coming on dark,
I said, Uncle John,
But I'll be along again,
Before very long.

Thanks for comin', he said,
To see Aunt Suze and me,
I'm not too bad, I s'pose,
For a hundred and three.

HARRY INGRAM

I guess at his age,
It's his right to complain,
And I really can't wait,
To go see him again.

My Great-Uncle John,
Is a very fine fella,
And if anyone asks,
I'll say, Let me tell ya . . .

Great-Uncle John? Don't be talkin'!

When our kids were small, they always asked us to lie down with them while they drifted off to sleep. It's been debated whether or not this was such a good idea. To us it was okay, and I believe it helped strengthen that special bond. Well, that is until things got a little out of hand.

Good Night Little One

I'll tell you a story,
A true one this time,
Of a pretty little girl,
With the prettiest smile.

She's the joy of my life,
And her sister is too,
But you have to be careful,
They'll turn on you.

Time for bed now,
Everyone up the stairs,
Get your teeth brushed,
And also your hair.

Slip on the jammies,
And into the bed,
Close them big eyes,
And lay down your head.

Oh, a beautiful sight,
I couldn't be more pleased,
As she looked up and smiled,
Daddy, can you lie down with me?

Without hesitation,
I smiled right back,
I lay down beside her,
It was time for *my* nap.

Not two seconds later,
She asked me so sweet,
Please, Daddy, a story,
I can't get to sleep.

So I took from the shelf,
I think, *Good Night Moon*,
But before I was finished,
She says, Can I watch cartoons?

So, I lay down the book,
And turned on the TV,
Not the smartest thing to do,
When you want them to sleep.

Five minutes, that's all,
You can't watch any more,

DON'T BE TALKIN'

But Daddy, she says,
I didn't see this one before.

So, half an hour later,
I turned off that thing,
Tried to settle her down,
And she asked me to sing.

And after a few lines of "Sarah,"
And "You Are My Sunshine,"
The eyes that were closing weren't hers,
They were mine.

Then out of nowhere,
I got to go pee!
So it was off to the bathroom,
That little girl and me.

Now all finished up,
And jammies back on,
I figured for sure now,
This won't take long.

So back into bed,
All safe and sound,
I looked over in shock,
At what I had found.

Her two little eyes,
Were finally closed,
I carefully got up,
Gave her a kiss on the nose.

Well, I heard a small voice,
As I entered the hall,
If she is the child,
Why was I starting to bawl?

Where are you going?
She quietly said,
I'm thirsty, I want a juice box,
No, milk instead!

So down to the kitchen,
I opened the fridge door,
To my horror I realized,
No milk. Oh, dear Lord!

I almost panicked,
At the thought of what's next,
I know, the wife is out,
I'll send her a text.

I headed back up,
To tell the bad news,
Thought of my wife,
Wished she were in *my* shoes.

But at the top of the stairs,
Not a sound did I hear,
She was sound to the world,
With her old teddy bear.

I smiled once more,
As I let out a sigh,

DON'T BE TALKIN'

Covered her up,
And wished her good night.

To watch your child sleep,
Is a beautiful thing,
But next time it's Mom's turn,
'Cause I need a drink.

A fun take on the classic mother-in-law, son-in-law rivalry. Believe it or not, she asked me to write it.

A Son-in-Law's Lament

I was just leaving work,
On that cold winter's day,
When a call came in,
And me wife she did say.

I slipped and fell,
On a hard patch of ice,
There's a bruise on my leg,
And it's not very nice.

It might be broken,
The wife said to me,
Now I'm no doctor,
But I had to agree.

So we went to emerg,
Now she's sporting a cast,
Me mind it was racing,
'Cause that won't heal fast.

My wife is so wonderful,
And looks after so much,
But what can she do,
With that cast and a crutch?

The thought crossed my mind,
I fair started to bawl,
Yes, here enters the story . . .
The mother-in-law.

I could move in,
She said with a smile,
Not for too long,
Just for a short while.

I rolled my eyes,
'Cause I knew by her voice,
The inevitable was coming,
And I had no choice.

Day one wasn't bad,
It was all pretty new,
The kids were excited,
And she even made stew.

But oh, what a taste,
I wouldn't feed to the cat,
Yes, the wife cooks much better,
Now that is a fact.

Heading out with the b'ys,
On day number four,

DON'T BE TALKIN'

To get a clean shirt,
Well, I opened the drawer.

The red one or white one,
Which one do you think?
Well she done the laundry,
So both options are pink.

And to turn on the TV,
Well, something was wrong,
I searched everywhere,
But the remote, it was gone.

Now where did she put it,
I know she's to blame,
I searched everywhere,
Trying to hold in my rage.

What day is it now?
Not even a week?
My nerves are shot,
I'm up to my peak.

Yes, I'm ready to snap,
Yes, my senses I'll lose,
If she doesn't leave soon,
I might start on the booze.

So I'm sitting at the pub,
Just having a few,
Since day fourteen,
It's a thing that I do.

When I heard a guy talking,
About his mother-in-law,
Saying how perfect she was,
Without any flaws.

He kept on going,
He was talking quite loud,
She's an angel, he said,
No one like her around.

You're lucky, I said,
She's not much like mine,
'Cause yours is an angel,
But mine's still alive.

The next night with the wife,
I was lying in bed,
When all of a sudden,
A thought entered my head.

The trip to the farm,
That's tomorrow, oh no,
The wife said, I can't walk,
But Mom can go.

Of course she can,
I nodded and grinned,
Smiling on the outside,
But inside I just cringed.

The kids will be thrilled,
They want her to go,

DON'T BE TALKIN'

I was dreading the trip,
With that crooked old crow.

Well, we got to the farm,
And the parking was great,
Parked three miles away,
To ensure we were late.

And my feet full of muck,
From this rainy wet weather,
Yes, I know it's winter,
But it's Newfoundland, remember.

We saw the small horses,
And saw the emu,
We saw the baby goats,
And the mother goat too.

We saw the donkey,
Who looked a bit cross,
He was bucking and kicking,
His back legs he tossed.

Now the mother-in-law,
Wasn't frightened at all,
She said he might be hungry,
The poor little doll.

She walked over close,
With a handful of hay,
But it wasn't the hunger,
I don't think, anyway.

HARRY INGRAM

With two feet and a kick,
As if right on cue,
The hay it went flying,
And the mother-in-law too.

It all turned out fine,
Even though it sounds bad,
I was in the knots,
While the kids helped their nan.

We went to the office,
To report the situation,
Showed off some bruises,
And a couple of abrasions.

I have just one question,
I asked the man there in charge,
He said I can't rent the donkey,
She's booked up 'til March.

So back home we went,
An adventurous day,
With the mother-in-law shook up,
But I guess she's okay.

She said, I think I'll go home now,
You don't need me,
Yes, the wife's doing better,
I quickly agreed.

She's finally gone,
After forty-three days,

DON'T BE TALKIN'

I guess it wasn't too bad,
I'll have to say.

Yes, I do have a soft spot,
For my mother-in-law,
It's out behind the house,
Next to the garage.

Christmas Is Here!

Christmas season's almost here,
From my childhood I remember,
That the tree went up two days before,
Not the middle of November.

Ho, ho, ho, Merry Christmas,
Jingle all the way,
Didn't we throw the pumpkin out?
It seems like yesterday.

Each year it's getting earlier,
It's really way too soon,
Sure, the Christmas tree will be blasty,
And for the nog you'll need a spoon.

Now I'm not being a Scrooge or Grinch,
Now don't be thinking that,
Just eat your Halloween candy,
Before you wear your Santa hat.

And I'm all for being on the ball,
I'll tell you that's a fact,
But the wife had all the presents bought,
Before the time went back.

Now it's not just the wife who is like it,
The stores are like it too,
October, I think they all start,
And I'll prove what I say is true.

While piecing together a costume,
For Halloween this year,
I had to rummage through the tinsel and bulbs,
To find a set of ears.

Now what if *all* the holidays,
Got earlier as well,
We'll have witches and goblins at Eastertime,
And God only knows what else.

Oh, what a tangled mess we'd have,
Would it ever be straightened out?
As each holiday got earlier,
Happy Hanukkah, St. Patrick would shout.

Santa would have to give up his suit,
And trade it for summer gear,
And the Easter Bunny'd be tipsy,
From St. Patrick's old green beer.

The groundhog would never see his shadow,
Cold weather he would shun,
And Cupid wouldn't shoot an arrow,
He'd have his moose to hunt.

And what if the Royal Regatta,
Were to change from what we know,

DON'T BE TALKIN'

They'd practise in the summer all right,
But on the frozen lake they'd row.

As each holiday got earlier,
It would cause us such a mess,
All because one neighbour,
Wanted his lights up before the rest.

So, I have just one more question now,
Before I take my leave,
Should auld acquaintance be forgot?
Please! Not 'til New Year's Eve.

This is quite possibly my favourite of all that I've written. Not only is it the first, but it's a tribute to my dad, the greatest man I've ever known.

Hands of Time

I watched him on that day as he left this world. I sat there holding his hand, watching him take his final breath. His hands were rough and callused from a lifetime of hard work.

From the moment we take our first breath, so begin the hands of time. There's something unseen and not often thought of, maybe even magical, in the touch of a hand.

From the first moment of life's journey, our hand is often placed in a parent's hand in comparison of size, but it's so much more than comparison. It's as if the strings of the heart extend all the way to our fingertips.

As more time passes, we meet so many along the way. Handshakes hold so many different meanings. It's a sign of respect when meeting an old friend or business associate. It is congratulatory for occasions like the birth of a child, a wedding, or any other of life's accomplishments. It is a gesture of condolence as we comfort others in the loss of a loved one.

I was nervous on the day when I held her hand while on bended knee. Then before I knew it, there we were, together at the altar, hands joined as one. "What God has joined together, let no man put asunder." A feeling I'll never forget.

We grow and learn as time travels forward. "Hold Dad's hand now," I say before crossing the street. I held my three-year-old daughter's hand as we jumped simultaneously from a four-inch-high curb. The simplest thing gave both of us much pleasure as we carefully made our way.

Tick tock, the hands of the clock move along, carrying us with them. So many emotions following with us as life's story unfolds. There's so much of this life's story left untold. It is with anticipation we watch as our sons and daughters continue to grow, making decisions that will affect their future, and even placing their hands into those of their chosen life partner as they prepare for their vows.

Life travels on and on, and eventually it will come full circle. As my circle continues, I reflect on that day. The day that his circle of life completed, and his hands of time stood still.

I watched him on that day as he left this world. I sat there holding his hand and watching him take his final breath. His hands were rough and callused from a lifetime of hard work.

Rest easy. You're home now, Dad.

During the 1960s, my dad and my uncle crossed the bay to build a house for their families as part of the resettlement program. They first built a henhouse, and then, while sleeping in the henhouse, built our home. The henhouse is featured in this true story of man vs. fox.

Fox in the Henhouse

Nineteen sixty-two,
I think was the year,
That Dad packed his stuff,
Yes, all of his gear.

With Mom and two kids,
He moved 'cross the bay,
For a far better life,
And a better day's pay.

In the heart of the bay,
In Arnold's Cove,
Not only a house,
Dad built a new home.

HARRY INGRAM

Now, I wasn't there,
It was before my time,
There were another four youngsters,
Before I saw the light.

How different was life,
Than that of today,
There wasn't much money,
So you found other ways.

With his garden there were many,
Potatoes to dig,
He had hens and a goat,
And also ten pigs.

Now, that is the setting,
To tell you the tale,
Of a man and a fox,
And who would prevail.

That big old henhouse,
He kept long ago,
With hundreds of hens,
He kept it just so.

From as far as Chance Cove,
And even Bellevue,
Then there was Come by Chance,
And Sunnyside too.

To buy the eggs,
There were dozens a day,

DON'T BE TALKIN'

Sold to the people,
Yes, they came a long way.

Now, that was the way,
For a couple of years,
'Til the hens they started,
To disappear.

Dad had his suspicions,
And it was no big shock,
When he found the culprit,
Was a dirty old fox.

To find a way,
To prevent this was tough,
But it had to be found,
Yes, enough was enough.

He tried to keep watch,
But with so much to do,
It was nearly impossible,
The frustrations grew.

So many hens,
What a horrible plight,
That fox, he kept stealing,
Each and every night.

'Til one morning my brother,
Was playing outside,
But then came in running,
With mouth open wide.

He was barely able,
To blurt the words out,
Fox in the henhouse!
He finally did shout.

With no time to delay,
Dad went for the door,
Yes, today was the day,
He could stand it no more.

With specific instructions,
For my brother to stand guard,
He left fear at the door,
And said, Keep the door barred.

What a ruckus and racket,
As you probably imagine,
With five hundred hens,
All cluckin' and clackin'.

The henhouse, it shook,
How the feathers they flew,
It was like something out,
Of a Bugs Bunny cartoon.

Then all of a sudden,
All things went quiet,
Not a sound could be heard,
Even the hens went silent.

Then the door shot open,
And Dad stepped outside,

DON'T BE TALKIN'

With a halfway grin,
He held up his prize.

It was finally over,
He'd be bothered no more,
Yes, the hens were all safe,
He closed the hennery door.

Well, he skinned that fox,
Hung the fur in a tree,
Displayed it so proud,
For the world to see.

And never was there ever,
A problem again,
No sign of a fox,
That delighted the hens.

Some say that foxes,
Are clever and sly,
And cunning and crafty,
But you'll seldom come by.

A man like my dad,
The craftiest around,
He battled that fox,
And beat him hands down.

Yes, what Dad learned that day,
He put to good use,
He never owned a gun,
But he still got his moose.

A fun little tale based on some things that may or may not have happened in Placentia Bay a few years back.

Just inside the Gate

Long ago in Newfoundland,
Yes, way back in the day,
A profession then existed,
It was quite the lucrative trade.

Not a lot took part in this,
Not many had the gumption,
But many availed because of it,
With alcohol consumption.

In case you haven't guessed it,
It's the art of smuggling booze,
Or contraband, or rum-running,
Whichever term you choose.

Because this all occurred at sea,
You had to own a boat,

Schooners loaded to the gunnels,
It's a wonder they could float.

So, here's a story of a skipper,
His name I should not say,
But I guess I could reveal to you,
He's from Placentia Bay.

No, I don't wish to give out his name,
Don't wish to take the flak,
So, for the purpose of this story,
Sure, I s'pose we'll call him Jack.

He started with his father,
And his other brothers three,
They started in the fishing smacks,
Learned life out on the sea.

They worked upon the Grand Banks,
The weather rough or fine,
And got ten cents a pound for fish,
For six weeks at a time.

Now, Jack's father owned a schooner,
And since the bay was dry,
They ran some trips to Saint Pierre,
For spirits, rum, and rye.

Now, imagine how popular you could be,
Among the drinkers in the bay,
You couldn't make a living there,
But if you wanted to earn your pay . . .

DON'T BE TALKIN'

You could fill 'er up in Saint Pierre,
Try not to raise suspicion,
And run that liquor to the States,
In the time of prohibition.

Now, the brothers weren't too fond of this,
With the chance of getting caught,
And with his father getting old,
Well, I guess Jack's fate was sot.

So, he ran the rum and made some cash,
With everything running smooth,
With a couple of b'ys who didn't mind risk,
He had a hearty crew.

The months rolled along, which turned into years,
They became quite the smugglers,
Many's a day they narrowly escaped,
The US Coast Guard cutters.

A tricky game they played to and fro,
In and out of international waters,
And then, on the north side, RCMP boats,
They prayed to the soul of their fathers.

One night they got home and all went ashore,
Nine cases of rum left on board,
With the Mountie cutters lurking around,
They figured they'd bring it ashore.

They woke in the morning to a pound on the door,
Come on and let me in,

I knows you're home, Jack, and I knows what you're at,
You're committin' a mortal sin.

Open up, Jack, I knows you got rum,
I heard it from one of the merchants,
The only thing left is the house now, Jack,
The boat and the stage, sure, I searched it.

Jack opened the door so it wouldn't be bet in,
Said, Come on in, b'ys, look around,
Look anywhere at all, the upstairs too,
I'm sure there's nothing to be found.

There's just one room at the top of the stairs,
Aunt Soph is in lying down,
They think she might have the consumption,
That dirty ol' stuff's goin' around.

They opened the door and had a quick peek,
Aunt Soph said, I'm not very well,
They closed the door and apologized to her,
She's certainly sick, I can tell.

Well, I guess that's it, the authorities said,
I guess we'll be on our way,
But I tell you, Jack, you know we'll be back,
And you'll be in jail someday.

Jack barred the door and bawled out to Soph,
Get up, girl, and clean off your face,
You'll have to scrub it good and hard,
Or that flour might turn into paste.

DON'T BE TALKIN'

I'll get the bottles from under the bed,
And hide them up in the loft,
We got away with another one, Soph,
But I think I'll soon call it off.

Yes, Jack had enough after ten or twelve years,
This one was way too close,
I'll give it all up for the sake o' me health,
And p'raps turn religious, I s'pose.

Well, that's what he did, he gave up the booze,
And turned to the church to repent,
Not a drop did he touch, to Aunt Soph's delight,
To prayers every Sunday he went.

I might still get to Heaven, he thought to himself,
The Good Lord will determine my fate,
For a seat on the throne, I don't really care,
As long as I'm inside the gate.

Well, he lived a long time, and he had a good life,
With children and grandkids as well,
His life running rum and avoiding the law,
He vowed that he never would tell.

His secret stayed hidden, not too many knew,
As Jack got on in years,
Now a kind-hearted soul who helped all that he could,
His conscience now it was cleared.

A couple of years later his health started failing,
Some might say he took sick,

But he'd lived a long life full of love and adventure,
When he passed it was painless and quick.

The wake was a time as you'd probably expect,
With lots of rum from Saint Pierre,
They all drank a toast to Captain Jack,
There's not one more soul could compare.

They went to dig the grave and found,
The cemetery was almost filled,
They dressed him up and laid him out,
Brought his pine box up the hill.

No one realized at the time,
But here's what proved Jack's faith,
The last one buried in the cemetery,
He was just inside the gate.

Sometimes we just need to stop and smell the roses.

Simple Things

Sat at the table,
Pen in my hand,
I factor the mortgage,
The house, and land.

Yes, there's bills to pay,
They pile up sometimes,
With the realization,
What I buy isn't mine.

The bank owns the lot,
Sometimes it's a mess,
With each passing payment,
It adds to the stress.

And the kids need to keep up,
With the other girls and boys,
They need clothes and shoes,
Not to mention the toys.

HARRY INGRAM

Yes, the family life adds,
Economic strain,
And sometimes it feels,
Like life is a pain.

But quite often we forget,
And I'm sure you'll agree,
That the greatest of pleasures,
Most often are free.

A walk in the park,
Won't cost you a cent,
If you sit on the swing,
Your wallet won't bend.

And to pick a few flowers,
The smell is so sweet,
To yarn with a friend,
Not a cent you will need.

To sit on a beach,
And hear the waves roar,
Or watch a bald eagle,
In the sky as it soars.

Or to wade in the water,
'Til you're out past your knees,
Yes, this, my friend,
Is enjoyable and free.

You can play a little tune,
If you're musically inclined,

DON'T BE TALKIN'

Or hum it or sing it,
It won't cost a dime.

And if you can't sing,
Don't worry at all,
Listening is free,
So heave back, have a ball.

There're people who spend,
Their whole entire lives,
Working and slaving,
Yes, trying to survive.

To keep up with the Joneses,
They spend every penny,
They work hard for their money,
But aren't left with any.

So, you can work all day,
To buy all your big toys,
Like quads and skidoos,
And other things that make noise.

But there's nothing more heartfelt,
You can take it from me,
Yes, a smile and a,
Daddy, I love you, is free.

A "kind of" true story of what happened when I tried, for the first time . . . insanity wings.

Hot Sauce

Allow me to relate,
A story that's spicy,
And I don't mean romantic,
Or anything dicey.

So, don't mind the youngsters,
Don't cover their ears,
It's a story of hot sauce,
That brought me to tears.

You see, whenever asked,
Do you like hot stuff?
I assumed they meant food,
And said, Can't get enough!

Now, that is a fact,
What I'm saying is true,
From the time I was ten,
I used Tabasco in stew.

And then came the peppers,
What a wonderful taste,
When your mouth starts to burn,
And red turns your face.

And then I continued,
For a few years or more,
With hot wings and chilis,
And hot sauce galore.

Then a friend of mine said,
They got these new things,
They're the spiciest ever,
Called *insanity wings*.

Now a little intrigued,
I said it can't be that bad,
So, I found the location,
Yes, they had to be had.

I walked in and sat down,
At the table I chose,
When a waiver they shoved,
Right in front of my nose.

No thank you, kind sir,
I don't want to sign,
That's probably for tourists,
You can keep mine.

Oh no, said the waiter,
You have to sign first,

DON'T BE TALKIN'

So, reluctantly I did,
But I was sure I'd had worse.

And then he continued,
To tell us the tale,
Of ten people or more,
Both female and male.

Who tried these wings,
They still come here, all right,
But two guys and three girls,
Have all lost their sight.

And one poor fella,
I don't remember his name,
Hiccupped after lunch,
And set the table ablaze.

And another young man,
Ate three while half-soused,
And lost all of the skin,
From the roof of his mouth.

But I didn't flinch,
I thought this must be lies,
So, bring on the food,
I'm gettin' hungry, I cried.

Well, not long after that,
To my table appeared,
A man in a suit,
Like the NASA crowd wears.

He set on the table,
An assortment of things,
Plus a gallon of milk,
And the insanity wings.

Saying, You might want to eat,
The other stuff first,
And drink half the milk,
Yes, prepare for the worst.

Well, I started in,
There's no time like the present,
As the waiter and staff,
Backed into the kitchen.

I could see them all peering,
From the window inside,
As I swallowed the first bite,
My eyes opened wide.

I couldn't feel a single,
Thing on my tongue,
And not only that,
My lips went all numb.

Saying, I won't let these wings,
Get the best of me,
I took a deep breath,
And gobbled down three.

Well, my vision went funny,
And I started to shake,

DON'T BE TALKIN'

Couldn't feel my fingers,
Or half of my face.

So, I went to the washroom,
For further inspection,
Well, my lips looked like,
They had Botox injections.

And the strength of this sauce,
Was making me cry,
Then a huge mistake . . . yes . . .
I wiped my eyes.

And oh, how they burned,
As they almost swelled shut,
And I was sure all the lining,
Had burned from my gut.

So, as I stood there in pain,
And also half blind,
I took a cramp in the stomach,
And then my behind.

Well, what happened next,
I'll spare you detail,
Yes, I'll leave that much out,
And continue the tale.

I went back to the table,
To pay for my meal,
Yes, forty-eight dollars,
What a hell of a deal.

So, let's take a look,
At what I got for my cash,
Swelled eyes and swelled lips,
And a permanent rash.

And my cast-iron stomach,
Now all burnt to cinders,
And I can hardly sit down,
'Cause my backside has blisters.

It's been quite a few years,
Since this all transpired,
When it comes to hot food,
Well, I guess I've retired.

No spices for me now,
I can't handle the taste,
Sure, all of my sauces,
Are now alfredo-based.

And I can't look at peppers,
Neither green nor red,
And with the thought of chili,
Comes a pain in the head.

So, if anyone should ask me,
Do you like hot stuff?
I say, No thank you kindly,
I think I've had enough.

This story is the true account of the year leading up to my wedding. Oh yes, and my wife's, too.

The Wedding That Almost Wasn't

"It's amazing we got married at all!" I said to my new bride jokingly. She didn't see the humour in quite the same way that I did. But once I assured her I was not serious at all, we both ended up having a fine laugh at the situation. Well, looking back at all that had transpired over the past year, she certainly understood the reason I had said it. We both gave each other a knowing look of, "I'm glad we got through it."

    It was a year or so before this that I brought her back to the same place we met. She thought we were there to celebrate her birthday. But the cake did not say happy birthday. It said the words that she'd been waiting to hear. I hurried to one knee, and in fine romantic style, I popped the question. There were so many tears of joy from us both as she happily agreed to marry me. We cut the cake and shared it with people sitting nearby who applauded our new engagement. We looked at each other knowing we would be together always. And so, the planning had begun.

We had so much to do, knowing how fast the year that followed would go. I wanted white invitations, she wanted beige. So, we got beige. I wanted the colour theme to be white and blue. She wanted white and purple. Well, it wasn't actually purple. It was lilac, whatever that is. To me, it was purple. Anyway, we had white and purple. She wanted a three-tier cake, and I wanted two. So, we got three. I'm so glad she wanted my input and that we worked as a team to make these decisions.

The third week into planning mode, we ordered lovely wedding invitations. It seemed to take forever for us to receive them, but finally the day arrived, and we were so excited. We ripped them open in a burst of excitement only to discover they were pink. Oh no. Wrong colour. Then we noticed a little something else that was incorrect. They were written in Portuguese! Upon closer investigation, we realized they were actually not our invitations at all. I wasn't quite sure who Albertina Hilario and Gilberto Lomba were, but I was sure they were lovely people and I wished them all the best in their upcoming nuptials. Strike one!

The planning continued with the big decision, the biggest one of all. She was deciding on a wedding dress. I wasn't allowed to have input into this one at all. This was all her. With her mom in tow, she went to every wedding shop in town and tried on every gown she could find. There were ones with big frilly bows, sequins, long trains, short trains, with and without veils, and even ones that you'd see a bride wearing on a street corner in Las Vegas. Thankfully she didn't pick that one. But what she did pick was something from a fairy tale. It was absolutely beautiful, so fitting for my bride-to-be. We happily returned home knowing one more thing could be scratched off the list. Done!

We went back to work with flower arrangements, guest lists, caterers, and all the other important things that needed to be sorted. About six weeks before the wedding, we were sitting back, enjoying the fact that pretty much all the planning had been done with only a few minor details to be sorted. I turned on the TV to scroll through the stations to see if there was anything interesting to watch. We noticed "Breaking News" from the downtown area. Always interested in any kind of current events, we watched to see what was going on. A fire was raging, wiping out three small businesses. One of which was . . . you guessed it. The very same wedding shop her wedding dress was in! This was *not* good. Strike two!

We tried to reach them that night, but no one was answering. I guess you couldn't really blame them. The next day we continued with call after frantic call, being met by answering machines and busy signals. Finally, someone picked up the line. The voice that greeted us wasn't a happy one. Some things were saved, but not a lot. The wedding dress she'd fallen in love with was gone.

But this didn't turn out all bad. They were insured, and we managed to find another dress she liked just as well. With the help of friends with connections, we got it fitted and altered with a couple of weeks to spare. Another bullet dodged.

Well, the day finally arrived, with both of us realizing how lucky we were to have made it. But there was really no way we couldn't have. We would have persevered through anything. She was in one waiting area, with me in the other. We were both full of anticipation with a touch of anxiety on the side for good measure. They were about to play "Canon in D." This was the song she selected for the walk down the aisle. Of course, I wanted "Here Comes the Bride," but we all know at this point how that went.

I took a deep breath, looked around at the guys I had chosen to share this day with, smiled, and reached for the doorknob. This was it. It was time to go wait for my bride. Then, all of a sudden . . . darkness! Yes, strike three, otherwise known as the power outage. I could hear the murmurs throughout the church, and a faint cry from a woman in the next room. It sounded like something I'd hear my father say after he stubbed his toe, or that time he got the fish hook caught in his hand. But that's another story. The woman using this colourful language was soon identified as my future wife.

I'm sure we were both thinking the worst, when suddenly the bridesmaids and groomsman sprang into action. It wasn't long before we had a friend playing the sweetest of melodies on his guitar and candles were lit. The only other sounds that could be heard were the rustle of clothing as people stood to watch the bride walk down the aisle and the gasps at how beautiful she looked. She wore a gorgeous dress and the brightest of smiles. We then said our vows in front of all. It turned out to be a perfect day.

For a wedding that almost wasn't, it turned out to be the finest wedding I had ever attended. But then again, I may be a little biased.

My Childhood Christmas

I tried so hard to get to sleep. I tried counting sheep, because that was the thing to do, but no. It didn't work for me. What to do next? I tried to create visions of sugar plums dancing in my head like the story says, but still nothing. My young body was tired. But there were so many thoughts of what the morning would bring.

A bike? No, it was winter, and besides, that would be way too big of a gift for Santa to bring. Maybe a board game, a Superman action figure, or . . . oh my, oh my, I'll never get to sleep, I thought. And with that, I nodded off for what seemed like no more than a minute when I jumped to my feet, only to realize that it was still dark. It was only 3:00 a.m. and my journey to dreamland began all over again. To be honest, I didn't get much sleep between then and daylight. And then, as the sun kissed the morning sky, I knew it was finally here. Merry Christmas! I jumped up and ran out the hall, yelling to everyone as I made my way, gazing under the tree to see what Santa had brought. Oh yes! A Superman action figure *and* a new tool kit. I couldn't believe Santa had brought me *two* things.

Then I spied my stocking, one of Dad's wool socks, blocked full of fruit and chocolate. Oh boy, now *this* is Christmas.

It wasn't long before Mom and Dad were up and in the kitchen and you could smell the bacon cooking. Mmm. Such a rare treat. Bacon and eggs. Well, you could have eggs whenever, but we only had bacon a couple of times a year, Christmas and Easter.

Then it was time for Dad to sing. He always sang an old favourite of ours: "One Christmas Morning Bill Bought a Gun." I was never too sure where it came from, nor had I heard anyone else ever sing it, but it was a tradition in our house, and we all enjoyed it.

Mom got the turkey on early for Christmas dinner, and Dad helped with the veggies. Before long, dinner was ready and all hands sat down for an amazing meal. I got a smack on the back of the hand for reaching out for a bit of turkey before Mom had set the table. (Still stings a bit just thinking about it.) Finally, she said grace, and all hands dug in.

After we finished, I wanted to play my sister's new Monopoly game. I got special permission from Mom as it was Sunday, because we all knew that there would be no playing games on Sunday. Not in our house, anyway.

The day progressed with visits from aunts, uncles, and grandparents bearing gifts, which mostly consisted of socks. Some were store-bought, but most were hand-knitted, and although you'd much rather something else, those socks sure kept your feet warm in the long cold nights in the winter.

Then came Christmas supper. Salads, turkey left over from lunch, cakes and red jelly and custard for dessert. You can't beat that. Oh yes, and the candles, I almost forgot. Our Christmas supper was always eaten by candlelight. That was the only meal of the year we did that, and even though you couldn't see real well, it gave Mom such a feeling of joy and happiness that it was worth missing your mouth the odd time, just to see her glow.

Ah yes, full of turkey and contentment, we waited for the day to close, watching a few Christmas shows on the old black and white TV. Then off to bed. That was a good one, all right. Just 364 more days until it all happens again. Merry Christmas!

Helping Hand

Wake up! Wake up! said the wife as she shook me,
There's somebody at the door,
Still half asleep, I looked at the clock,
Three a.m., I soon rolled back o'er.

But she didn't stop, Come on, get up,
You don't know who it could be,
It could be my mother, out stuck in a ditch,
I just smiled and went back to sleep.

Then a pillow I got in the side of the head,
That brought me right to my feet,
I'll go downstairs and check, I s'pose,
I wondered who it could be.

Still half asleep with my bathrobe on,
It's down the stairs I went,
With the doorbell ringing and knock knock knocking,
You'd think there was somebody dead.

When I opened the door I got quite the surprise,
As a man stood there swaying,
And a powerful smell of the pub nearby,
Saying words like you do when you're praying.

Can I help you? I asked, Are you all right?
It's 3:00 a.m. don't you know,
I was wondering, he slurred, if you'd give me a push,
I could really use it, he croaked.

And that's what I'm not, I angrily said,
Go on 'fore I call the police,
You smell like booze and you're not fit to drive,
And I'm going back to sleep.

I slammed the door and went back upstairs,
As the wife she quickly sat up,
What was that all about? she worriedly asked,
Some drunk from the local pub.

He was wanting a push, can you imagine that,
A push! at this time of night,
And the stench of booze you could smell for miles,
And no police in sight.

Oh come on now, sure, it's not all bad,
Don't you remember that time?
The time we were at the wedding last fall?
When you had three glasses of wine?

I had to drive your big ole truck,
And the gears were so hard to switch,
I stopped to look down, not used to a standard,
And we ended up in the ditch.

Half down in a ditch with me in my dress,
And you in a rented tux,

DON'T BE TALKIN'

Aren't you glad those young fellas stopped?
We couldn't believe our luck.

They pushed us out and saved our night,
Now, think about that for a second,
Yes, think about that poor man outside,
This is a valuable lesson.

I thought for a minute and couldn't dispute,
Yes, all that she said was right,
I quickly got dressed and put on my boots,
To venture out into the night.

Well, I opened the door, and all was dark,
The night was just like the pitch,
I wondered if he was out of gas,
Or maybe down in a ditch.

Hello! I called, Is anyone there?
Yes, I'm over here!
I tried to pick out his shape in the dark,
I yelled out, Over where?

Do you still need a push? I then bawled out,
I had a change of heart, I guess,
Oh, bless you, he said, I certainly do,
I'm over here . . . on the swing set.

The Square Root of Pie

Marg's bakery! Come get your doughnuts,
Sold by the each or the dozen,
We serve coffee and tea and muffins and cookies,
And pies right out of the oven.

Now, this was the ad that Marg used for years,
She supplied the whole town with sweets,
But one fateful day, things took a turn,
Poor Marg had to call the police.

Someone broke in and stole all the pies.
It's a mystery, no one knows why,
Or how many were robbed, so to figure that out,
They just multiplied by pi.

They stole them all, there were rhubarb pies,
And other ones made with cream cheese,
And strawberry, apple, and lemon meringue,
And pumpkin ones for Halloween.

Not one pie left as Marg read her statement,
It's a travesty, what do I do now?
The sergeant said not to worry about it,
They'd figure out the why and how.

And the who, of course, they'd solve this dilemma,
And put the crook in the clink,
But in the meantime, there are still lots of doughnuts,
And tea and coffee to drink.

Marg agreed but was still pretty flustered,
And was certainly not amused,
But then asked the cop in a concerning tone,
Will this story be on the news?

Oh, indeed it will, the policeman replied,
It will help us to get information,
And it won't be long before everyone knows,
All about your situation.

Well, the days passed by and still not a word,
They decided to call off the search,
But by this time Marg wasn't bothered at all,
Things had gotten better, not worse.

It seems that the story had travelled really fast,
With the town being relatively small,
Next morning there were dozens lined up at the shop,
Poor Marg almost started to bawl.

She was so very thankful now business was booming,
Not long getting back on track,
It actually seemed better, her sales through the roof,
All this kindness she could never pay back.

Marg was delighted, her plan worked quite well,
Oops! her plan? Did I say that out loud?

DON'T BE TALKIN'

Well, she told me all about it and, well,
I said I wouldn't tell, I vowed.

Well, I guess that's it, I might as well tell ya,
Now that I've spilled all the beans,
And since this happened, it was ten years or more,
So she probably wouldn't mind coming clean.

She was the culprit, it was her all along,
See, her business was struggling indeed, sir,
So, to get the attention and a spot on the news,
She hid all the pies in her freezer.

So, if you're in the market to purchase a bakery,
She might sell you the store and supplies,
But I wouldn't trust her or give her a job,
And always keep your eye on the pies.

And to get the word out you can buy TV ads,
Or hire a publicity agent,
But if you want results, just call the cops,
And hide all your pies in the basement.

This particular story has a very personal connection to me. It came to light after a visit with my Aunt Ruby. She told me the tragic tale of my great-great-uncle and his wife, but also how true love can reign over tragedy. It was a story that had been passed down through a couple of generations. After the visit, I decided to do a little research. I found some information on the events that took place. So, using the words of my dear aunt and a newspaper article or two, I filled in the blanks and brought the story to life.

Mildred and Mose

One summer's evening, Mildred and Mose lay in grass in Hayes Meadow. They gazed up into the starry night. Their minds were wandering with dreams of the future. They knew they would be together forever. They talked of the wedding, and how it would probably be in January, but only if they could put enough away by then. See, Mose was a fisherman, and with squarin' comin' in the fall, there was no guarantee. But there was always hope.

    Well, fall came and went, and once the merchant got his share, as expected, there was very little money left. But when they looked at it, at least they weren't gone in the hole like other years. And the berries were plentiful. And they had fish salted away and a good many potatoes, so they decided to get married after all.

So, one day early January, the tenth, I believe, they got dressed in their Sunday, goin' to meetin' clothes, and off to the church they went. There they said their "I dos," and it was off to the Hall for the supper. What a feed. Lots of grub on the go. Mildred's family had made away with one of their sheep and sent it around to all the women in Muscle Harbour Arm to make boilers of mutton soup. And quite the few boilers turned up, too. This big feast, of course, was followed by the time. Mac played the accordion 'til near daylight, with all hands out for the square dance.

Now, about a week later, it was time for the honeymoon. Most couples could hardly afford anything extravagant like that, and half probably didn't even know what it was, but Mildred and Mose were off to Nova Scotia to celebrate the beginning of their new life together.

They packed a trunk, as was common back then. No one had a suitcase. They boarded the boat and headed for Arnold's Cove, where they would catch the train. Once they arrived, they were seated in separate cars. It didn't matter, married or not, there was a car for the women and a car for the men. With no electricity, on the dark evenings of the winter, these cars were lit by kerosene lamp, which were hung on the walls of each car.

The train pulled from the station and travelled for a few hours. Those few hours seemed like days to these two as they longed for each other's company.

Soon, night came upon them, and so too did their slumber. But this sea of dreams was cut short. Just as the sun was about to meet the morning sky, a loud screeching noise could be heard throughout the train. Then with one great motion, both cars holding these two young lovers jumped the rails and overturned just outside Glenwood.

A fire soon broke out and began spreading rapidly because the kerosene lamps had been overturned and smashed. While Mose's car wasn't burning quite so badly, he managed to make it to safety. Through all the screams and cries for help, he could hear his name being called. Having nothing left to live for without his one true love, he made his way to the flame-engulfed structure. His voice now raspy from drawing smoke with every breath, Mose called her name, and Mildred called his.

With the sun high in the sky the next morning, what a horrific sight was found by the rescue crew. There were many fatalities that morning. Among these were the bodies of Mildred and Mose, lying together, with not even death able to part them.

Although a tragic end, no greater love story could ever be told. The story of Mildred and Moses Rodway, who fell in love at an early age and vowed they'd spend the rest of their days together . . . so, too, did they make good on their promise. The promise from that summer's evening in the grass in Hayes Meadow.

Further to the story, the events herein, in part, were responsible for the removal of kerosene lamps from the walls of the train cars in the Newfoundland Railway system in the early 1900s. Mildred's trunk can be found at the Railway Coastal Museum in St. John's, NL.

Don't Ask

You know, being a parent,
Sometimes you don't know,
If you're doing it right,
So you go with the flow.

Like a little while back,
About a month or two,
I was fixing the mower,
Or at least trying to.

When a voice behind me,
Made me quite perplexed,
As my eight-year-old daughter asked,
Daddy, what's sex?

Once I realized for sure,
This wasn't a joke,
I couldn't decide first,
A heart attack or stroke.

Yes, this is my daughter,
And she's only eight,
I thought ten years for sure,
Before her first date.

Let alone asking questions,
Like this one, you see,
It's way too soon,
For the birds and the bees.

Times, how they changed,
Since I was that age,
Even saying the "S" word,
Would put Dad in a rage.

Of course, I had four sisters,
But enough about that,
I'll get back to the story,
So there I sat.

Well, I've been a good dad,
Up to this point, I guess,
So, I sat down beside her,
And tried my best.

First, I thought *lies!*
That's the way out of this,
You see, my dear daughter,
It's a type of fish.

That didn't work,
She just looked at me funny,
No, I meant to say lion,
No, zebra . . . no, monkey!

Well, she called me out,
Said, Dad, you're not fooling me,

DON'T BE TALKIN'

I'm practically a grown-up,
I'm in grade three.

The further it went,
The worse I got,
I stuttered and stammered,
Cleared my throat a lot.

I thought I'd give in now,
And let it all go,
And tell her stuff,
She probably shouldn't know.

You see, there are boys and there are girls,
And when they like each other,
Well, they will grow up,
To be fathers and mothers.

I continued on,
With some minor detail,
But my heart was pounding,
As she sat there and stared.

I even told her the rhyme,
About the space and the string,
You know the one,
I remember, I think.

When God made boys, He made them out of string,
He had some left over, so He left a little thing,
When God made girls, He made them out of lace,
He didn't have enough, so he left a little space.

HARRY INGRAM

Well, I tried my hardest,
To continue this tale,
But I thought it's time to give up,
Yes, this time I failed.

But before our talk ended,
I said, Now listen here, miss,
Why in the world,
Would you ask about this?

Well, she still seemed a little,
In shock from my words,
Not expecting a story,
About bees and birds.

She said, Mom said to come out,
Now, listen to what's next,
She said, Supper will be ready,
In a couple of secs!

Labour disputes at the North Pole are never fun.

Havoc at the North Pole

'Twas early October,
Up at the North Pole,
Months of preparing,
Had taken their toll.

The oldest of the bunch,
Were both tuckered out,
Yes, Donner and Blitzen,
I'm talking about.

All tired out,
From years of hard work,
Both getting older,
Joints starting to hurt.

At the annual meeting,
They developed a plan,
For when Santa gets back,
From Newfoundland.

He's gone for a visit,
He'll be back before long,
Perhaps get a moose,
If hunting season's on.

Time quickly passed,
And the CEO returned,
He was there to address,
All their cares and concerns.

The elves all turned up,
And the reindeer too,
Mrs. Claus laid out food,
For the whole entire crew.

They talked about training,
And their level of fitness,
And maximizing the gift,
Distribution business.

They addressed global warming,
And weather conditions,
And the reindeers' diet,
To cut back on emissions.

Donner spoke up, and said,
Me and Blitzen,
Are both nearing the age,
Of senior citizens.

Then Blitzen spoke,
After finishing some cabbage,

And suggested an early,
Retirement package.

All hands went mad,
Things started to unravel,
Santa shouted for order,
As he banged down his gavel.

But they didn't listen,
They all had their gripes,
All started talking,
With no end in sight.

Then Dasher spoke up,
And talked of bad dreams,
Of how Santa turned angry,
Yes, downright mean.

So, a fear of Santa,
You might say he has,
Or Claus-trophobia,
It's also known as.

Comet interrupted,
And proceeded to tell us,
That from grazing on tinsel,
He now has tinselitis.

And then there was Rudolph,
Leader of the pack,
Said his nose was fading,
Sure, it's almost gone black.

With the elves overworked,
They had their say too,
We want recognition,
For all that we do.

An increase in wages,
And fringe benefits,
Or we all go on strike,
Conditions are not fit.

Calm down now, b'ys,
St. Nick yelled for order,
We'll call in a mediator,
Yes, I will inform her.

It's only to call,
I know she'll be here,
You might know her,
It's Olive, the other reindeer.

To help with the issues,
She quickly agreed,
And after debriefing,
She was now up to speed.

She took Santa and Rudolph,
And behind closed doors,
A private meeting was held,
For three hours or more.

They emerged from the room,
All wearing big smiles,

A new reindeer contract,
They held up with pride.

To fix all the problems,
Was a challenge, said Olive,
But I'm sure you'll be happy,
And that I can promise.

The first thing addressed,
Was Dasher's bad dreams,
She said, I know it sounds scary,
But to me it just seems.

Like you need visions of sugar plums
Dancing in your head,
So she gave him a book to read,
Just before bed.

'Twas the night before Christmas,
She read it out loud,
And soon Dasher was sleeping,
Not making a sound.

And for Comet's ailing throat,
No need for physicians,
These candy canes are magic,
They'll restore mint condition.

And since he couldn't tell,
A green tree from blasty,
An operation for Rudolph,
Yes . . . rhinoplasty.

Then she turned her attention,
To the elves and their crew,
For extra hours worked,
They get time off in lieu.

An increase in wages,
Is that what you say?
Free candy on Sundays,
Plus two dollars a day.

With that figured out,
The last thing on the list,
Was Donner and Blitzen,
And how they'd be missed.

All agreed they couldn't quit,
Couldn't go anywhere,
They were part of the team,
And had been for years.

To resolve this issue,
Well, Santa had a plan,
He bought a used motor,
From an old 12 Elan.

In Newfoundland, it was,
On the last trip he made,
He bought it outright,
From a fella named Dave.

That could power the sled,
Through the rain, sleet, and snow,

DON'T BE TALKIN'

With the reindeer relaxing,
They'd be there just for show.

All hands started cheering,
And shouting hurray,
They couldn't wait for Christmas,
And the new powered sleigh.

They thanked Olive for her service,
And went back to work,
They were all excited,
For their new gifts and perks.

Everything's all right now,
Their problems all cleared,
They all hoped they wouldn't,
Need Olive next year.

So she galloped and galloped,
Until her legs soon took flight,
Merry Christmas, everyone,
And to everyone good night!

Back in 2018, I read an article about a local seniors' home that was so touching it inspired the following.

Three Stones

From the big picture window at the top of the hill,
He gazed out 'cross the bay,
His mind was at home, and days not long ago,
But illness had brought him this way.

He's not quite as young as he used to be,
No life so quickly drifts by,
But through happiness and tears, for thirty-six years,
Jack had true love right by his side.

Every morning she arrived at the home,
And was greeted by a hug and a grin,
As his mind it did drift, it sure gave him a lift,
Mary brought home there to him.

A gentle old soul he'd been all his life,
And quite the hard worker as well,

HARRY INGRAM

He worked big machines and still does in his dreams,
By the feel of his hands you could tell.

He was always so kind with a gentle demeanour,
He never had a very sharp tongue,
He wouldn't utter a curse, or anything worse,
Sure, that's what kids do when they're young.

But when he was asked about life's regrets,
It came as a bit of a surprise,
There's one I can think, and at Mary he winked,
I didn't get to make her my bride.

They shared every day by each other's side,
Why would anyone think they weren't wed?
No one had a clue, that in fact it was true,
Through the years, no vows they were said.

The staff and the friends of this couple in love,
Knew exactly what had to be done,
With excitement they spoke, with all taking notes,
And soon, their plan had begun.

I know a florist, one woman said,
And I'm sure she'll help where she can,
And then another got a dress from her mother,
And fitting and sewing began.

Then the tailor shop's brother heard of the plan,
Yes, he knew them both very well,
They donated the suit, with the vest and the shoes,
For this giving there was no parallel.

DON'T BE TALKIN'

The day it drew nearer, the plan was in place,
Like a puzzle it all came together,
He'd call her his wife, the love of his life,
In three days no matter the weather.

Oh, one more surprise, the therapist, you see,
He was working with Jack all the while,
And for the first time in years, he stood there with tears,
To watch his bride walk down the aisle.

A great time was had as they said their "I dos,"
For happiness, this couldn't be outdone,
That day at the home, he gave a ring with three stones,
As they both joined together as one.

The long day ended, the excitement died down,
The months, they quickly rolled on,
She still visits each day and by his side stays,
With good fortune they've been shined upon.

As time passes by, an anniversary approaches,
It'll be two years this December,
With their minds free of care and the love that they share,
With kindness she helps him remember.

They remember their youth and how they first met,
The good times and the bad times there too,
And oh yes, one more thing, he remembers the ring,
And how the three stones mean "I love you."

From the big picture window at the top of the hill,
They gaze out across the bay,

HARRY INGRAM

The tale now it's told of love purer than gold,
With this love growing stronger each day.

This is kind of a sequel to "Don't Be Talkin'." Some say it has more of a prequel feel.

The Fair

The Fair! Aunt Suze bawled,
As she looked at the paper,
Can we go this year, John?
It's the fifteenth of April.

Humph! said Uncle John,
A money racket, I s'pose,
Sure, we already went,
Was it ten years ago?

Oh, come on now, John,
I'm sure you'll have fun,
They got all kinds of games,
And stuff to be won.

They've got the Tiptop and Scrambler,
And all kinds of rides,
It's at the old Target,
Down on Stavanger Drive.

Well, he hemmed and he hawed,
And didn't want to go,
'Til Aunt Suze noticed something,
He couldn't say no.

Helicopter rides,
They do all sorts of tricks,
Even go upside down,
Do dives and flips.

He sat up in his chair,
With a half-raised eyebrow,
It'll cost a small fortune,
But we'll go anyhow.

In a couple of short weeks,
The day had arrived,
Aunt Suze hates the traffic,
So Uncle John had to drive.

They got to the fair,
And oh my what a crowd,
Half the island is here,
Said Uncle John, I 'lows.

The balloon game with darts,
Was the first thing Suze saw,
Let's play this one, John,
You can win a stuffed dog.

And how much is that?
A dollar, you knows,

DON'T BE TALKIN'

A dollar is a dollar,
But we'll do it, I s'pose.

They continued on,
But didn't win a thing,
Then Aunt Suze saw the game,
With the pegs and the rings.

And this one was worse,
Two dollars to play,
And two dollars is two dollars,
But they played anyway.

Now, you can't say they lost,
On this one at all,
They won the small prize,
The cup, string, and ball.

With each game and each ride,
The prices got higher,
Aunt Suze played the games,
With Uncle John right beside her.

They got in the strawberries
That twirl 'round and 'round,
Uncle John got half sick,
Thought he'd have to lie down.

Not to mention the fright,
They shouted and hollered,
There's a lot better ways,
To spend nearly five dollars.

Well, on they went,
With more rides and more games,
With his pension cheque gone,
John thought what a shame.

And a waste of time,
And money too,
I'm just about froze,
Said Uncle John to Aunt Suze.

And me feet are right sore,
From all of this walkin',
Is it really that bad?
John said, Yis, don't be talkin'.

Just then he spied it,
Just like in the paper,
Helicopter rides,
This could be the saviour.

Yes, the trip it was sove,
It would be quite nice,
Now, now, said Suze,
Did you look at the price?

Fifty dollars is fifty dollars,
She promptly did say,
Uncle John just turned red,
Didn't know whether to swear or pray.

Well, you had your fun,
He said to Aunt Suze,

DON'T BE TALKIN'

And now it's my turn,
So you can't refuse.

Well, they argued a bit,
They weren't one bit quiet,
'Til their voices travelled,
To the nearby pilot.

Now, he liked his fun,
And he knew he couldn't lose,
So he proposed a bet,
To Uncle John and Aunt Suze.

He said to them both,
If you get in my chopper,
And you don't make a sound,
It won't cost a copper.

Well, Uncle John was delighted,
Couldn't wait for the ride,
He'd still get to go.
And save money on the side.

They started ascending,
The wind blowing their hair,
Aunt Suze feared for her life,
With Uncle John not a care.

They got up so high,
And they started to spin,
By this time the pilot,
Was sure he would win.

But still not a sound,
From either of the two,
I'll have them for sure,
With the next thing I do.

They started to drop,
And near hit the ground,
And then a full circle,
Yes, all the way around.

Well, he tried all he could,
With the ride winding down,
It was all he could do,
But still not a sound.

As the blades slowed down,
The pilot, he sighed,
I guess it's no charge,
I must say I'm surprised.

How did you do it?
It's a mystery to me,
Well, said Uncle John,
You might not believe.

When Suze fell out,
I almost give in,
But fifty dollars is fifty dollars,
He said with a grin.

The Lobster Tale

Now, Officer Jack was a fine old soul,
Respected by one and all,
But he wasn't a cop of any kind,
No, he wasn't a policeman at all.

Well, I guess respected is a bit of a stretch,
Probably more like tolerable,
See, the kind of an officer that Officer Jack was,
Was the local Fisheries Officer.

Now, the main occupation in this part of the bay,
Was the fishery, it kept them afloat,
Codfish and crab and lobsters to boot,
Sure, everyone owned a boat.

Things always ran smooth in this little town,
With everyone following the rules,
'Til young Jimmy Dicks got a little bit bored,
Always acting the fool.

But this story started with Officer Jack,
And don't worry, I'm not done with him yet,
He ties into the story along the way,
You see, Jimmy was proposed a bet.

HARRY INGRAM

This bet was to poach a lobster or two,
And try not to get caught in the process,
And if he didn't succeed in the time they agreed,
He'd be sporting his mother's nightdress.

Well, Jimmy agreed he was up for the sport,
He was down to the wharf that night,
He rigged up a lobster pot with two fathom of rope,
But a buoy was nowhere in sight.

Yes, nowhere in sight, it couldn't be seen,
Until the very next night at low tide,
Young Jimmy went down to haul up the pot,
Under cover of darkness at night.

And to his surprise on that very first haul,
Two of the finest lobsters you'd find,
A smile so wide came across his face,
He couldn't wait to show the b'ys.

The coast was clear as he shoved them,
Into a backpack on his back,
Turned around, and face and eyes,
Into . . . you guessed it . . . Officer Jack.

Ha, ha, he said, I've got you now,
I've been waiting for this moment forever,
You thought that you were much smarter than me,
But I am far more clever.

So, let's take a look, he proudly said,
With his flashlight right in Jim's eyes,

DON'T BE TALKIN'

Aha! he said, I knew it was lobsters,
Oh yes, said Jim, some size!

To the fullest extent of the law, says Jack,
You'll be punished, I guarantee,
And that's what I won't! You see, these are my pets,
Said Jimmy without skipping a beat.

Don't think I'm a fool, said Officer Jack,
I've never even heard of pet lobsters,
Now hand them over immediately, you see,
I'm the Fisheries Officer.

Hold on now, said Jim, I can prove it, he says.
Yes, I'll prove what I'm saying is right,
You see, I was just taking them for a swim,
Which they much prefer doing at night.

I go down to the wharf, I put them in,
And whistle a little while after,
It's then they come back and crawl up the slip,
Poor Jack almost died from laughter.

So, Jimmy sat down and let them go,
And waited ten minutes or more,
Officer Jack thinks now it's time,
For these lobsters to come back ashore.

Well, whistle, he said, for the lobsters to come,
Get them out of the water,
Jimmy turns and politely says,
What do you mean? Lobsters . . . what lobsters?

Now, Officer Jack might have gotten fooled,
But since then he's wise to all tricks,
You can't pull the wool over Officer Jack's eyes,
Well . . . unless you're young Jimmy Dicks.

Home to Stay

He sits on his couch,
All full of smiles,
Looks around at the clutter,
Of old and new toys.

Now, why the big smile,
I'll say it this way,
He now lives at home,
Yes, he came home to stay.

For years it was different,
A single young man,
He worked so hard,
With money to be had.

The thirst for knowledge,
And prosperity too,
As time quickly passed,
It was just work and school.

And finally receiving,
The grandest reward,
A job on the mainland,
He was so overjoyed.

HARRY INGRAM

Yes, he'd be away,
A month at a time,
But with all that he learned,
He'd rake in a pile.

And now with a wife,
They weren't married long,
And a child on the way,
She was three months along.

Oh, what a blessing,
He happily thought,
With a new family coming,
We won't be in want.

The finest big house,
With a two-car garage,
He left with a smile,
But his plan has its flaws.

It all seemed so perfect,
For the first little while,
With the thoughts of his family,
He carried a smile.

The months rolled along,
He could hardly wait,
The baby's soon coming,
And her name would be Kate.

A girl! he said,
And she looks like me,

DON'T BE TALKIN'

With tears of joy,
He stared at the screen.

It wouldn't be long,
Yes, he'd soon be there,
To hold his wife,
And young Kate so dear.

His time at home,
Was just a few days,
Then his job, it was calling,
Back up away.

As the months came and went,
He missed her first tooth,
He missed her first steps,
And her first taste of food.

With all that he missed,
It saddened him so,
Is this really life?
I really don't know.

His wife was so kind,
And caring and such,
But it had to be hard,
She missed him so much.

Sometimes she'd get angry,
And more times just sad,
As she raised this child,
Most times without Dad.

He watched all the videos,
Of her young life so far,
He was there all he could,
This was so very hard.

Now, sometimes in life,
It takes one final straw,
To make the decisions,
That help us along.

The video arrived,
Like all others do,
But this one was special,
She was just turning two.

She had a beautiful dress,
As she stood by her cake,
Then she blew out her candles,
And this she did say.

A wish for my daddy,
I miss you today,
I wish for my daddy,
To come home to stay.

He made up his mind,
And spoke to his boss,
There's no dollar value,
On the things that I've lost.

His next trip home,
Would be his last,

DON'T BE TALKIN'

With his job up away,
Now a thing of the past.

A new job back home,
A trade-off, all right,
His family together,
Each and every night.

Yes, he sits on his couch,
All full of smiles,
Looks around at the clutter,
Of old and new toys.

Now, why the big smile?
I'll say it this way,
He's pleased to be home,
Yes, he's come home to stay.

The One about the Pig

Writing stories is not too bad,
But naming them can be kind of hard,
You can't just pull a name out of the air,
Or dig it up in the backyard.

So, I put on my thinking cap and tried real hard,
Through my mind I started to dig,
So this recitation is affectionately known,
As "The One about the Pig."

I went to visit a friend of mine,
One I hadn't seen in years,
He's married now with a couple of kids,
But kind of an odd career.

I know people who work on computers,
Musicians playing gigs,
I know a doctor, a pilot, and a couple of teachers,
And one who raises pigs.

Yes, raising pigs, you heard me right,
He must have ten or a dozen,
He fattens them up and sells them off,
Except for his favourite, he loves 'im.

HARRY INGRAM

Other pigs just came and went,
With this one not forsaken,
This pig that he holds in such high regard,
He named Sir Francis Bacon.

He always was a happy pig,
Even in times of trouble,
Sure, one time he even got laryngitis,
And never became disgruntled.

But there was something peculiar about him,
And maybe you won't believe me,
'Cause the only pigs that I've ever seen have four legs,
But this one had three.

My curiosity got the best of me,
So I had to ask why,
He seemed to elude the question a bit,
Said I'll tell you by and by.

Some pig, that is, he said to me,
I thinks the world over him,
I remember the day I got 'im,
I was feeling kind of grim.

I thought a pig would help me, he said,
With no companion in my life,
Well, the one that sold that pig to me,
Sure, she became my wife.

Loves that pig, I do.

DON'T BE TALKIN'

But what about the leg, I asked,
But he didn't heed me at all,
It was about three years ago,
October, in the fall.

Four o'clock in the morning,
With pig squeals I was awakened,
I woke to find the house on fire,
All I could smell was bacon.

Well, Francis, I mean, he was next to me,
Making sure that me and the wife,
Both woke up and got out of the house,
He surely saved our lives.

B'y, that's some pig.

I get it, I said, You love the pig,
But now can you explain it to me,
How that pig only has three legs . . .
How that came to be.

Just stop and listen to me, he said,
I promise to fill you in,
I was down on the wharf, right down on the dock,
I was going for a swim.

As I dove my foot caught around a rope,
That was tied around the gump,
And you know I'm not the most agile,
In fact, I'm a little bit plump.

"I dangled over the edge, not touching,
The water nor the wharf,
Now, how was I getting out of this,
I started to brainstorm.

If I yell real loud, would someone hear?
I wondered what were the chances,
But then came running towards me,
Was that wonder sow named Francis.

Chewed through the rope and of course I fell,
But, sure, I was no worse off,
I hugged that pig, almost gave him a kiss,
Even put extra food in his trough.

Oh my, what a pig.

I was half-impressed and half-annoyed,
With the other half-tormented,
And if I don't hear the rest of this story,
Sure, I'll never be contented.

Okay, okay, he finally said,
I'll tell you, if you insist,
But the story is kind of like the pig,
The tale, it has a twist.

You ask me why he has three legs,
And why he's a favourite of mine,
Well, he said, a pig like that,
You can't eat all the one time.

Some pig.

Great-Uncle John's Christmas

'Twas a fortnight before Christmas, or something like that,
In a tiny house down in the cove,
The smoke swirled up from the chimney,
With a fine heat from the wood stove.

Sat in the corner with a scowl on his face,
By the stove sat me Great-Uncle John,
Christmas, he said, Is that here again?
I s'pose the crowd'll turn up before long.

They certainly will, Aunt Suze spoke up,
I can't wait to see the boys,
And the grandkids, John, there's three of them now,
Oh my, how the time flies.

We have to run out and buy all the gifts,
The toys and the sleds and the clothes,
Oh, isn't it a magical time of year?
John simply said, Humph, I s'pose.

Oh, and John? Don't forget the tree.

A good one, John, don't forget that,
I wants a nice tall one this year,

Not like that plastic one Margie got,
That she bought from Simpson Sears.

And the lights for the eaves, we need them put up,
And a new Christmas tablecloth too,
Sure, we had the last one for twenty-odd years,
I think that it's time we bought new.

The walls are all scrubbed, and the floors are done too,
And bedsheets are out on the line,
They'll be dried by this evening, I s'pose,
As long as the weather stays fine.

The cookies are done and me cakes are all made,
Except this one is missing a piece,
Was that you, John? Did you take a slice?
I am saving them for Christmas Eve.

I took it, Suze, I didn't think you'd mind,
In fact, I thought you'd be grateful,
I cut the right size and shoved it under,
The wobbly leg of the table.

John soon got up and went outside,
And made his way to the shed,
He dug out the lights that were rolled in a ball,
And the Santa, reindeer, and sled.

And then he heard, Oh, John! The tree, remember?

He got the decorations for inside the house,
Yes, every Christmas thing he could find,

DON'T BE TALKIN'

He took out the bulbs and ornaments,
With tinsel from eight years combined.

Now he broke the frilly thing that hangs on the wall,
You know, the one with the gold and red strips?
With John's lack o' learning and the letters reversed,
It now reads "Tmas Merry Chris."

He started the lights and swore all the while,
It's the same thing every year,
Bah, humbug! I think was an understatement,
'Tis a wonder he still got his hair.

Just then he heard it, the horns were blowing,
The youngsters screamin' quite loud,
They must have been carrying all that they owned,
As they headed up to the house.

The racket from the kids would wake the dead,
With the littlest one screechin' and bawlin',
And the other ones moaning about no Internet,
And how having no wi-fi is appalling.

John helped with the stuff, got them all squared away,
Then headed back out to the shed,
Right then Suze called out again,
Just to keep the thought in his head.

Not forgetting the tree, are ya, John?

He figured 'twas time to look for a tree,
Or Suze'd never let him relax,

So he told young John to come on and help,
Then he grabbed his bucksaw and axe.

Now, young John loved to spend time with his pop,
He was just about ten years old,
He loved the way he would yell and complain,
And all the stories he told.

They finally reached the top of the hill,
Inspecting each tree that they found,
Some were too short, and more were too tall,
And half were too big on the round.

Uncle John started grumblin', said, There's nar one no good,
He was just about at his wit's end,
Then little John looked up with a smile on his face,
And caught Uncle John holt by the hand.

He said that's okay, Pop, sure we got all day,
That smile was so bright and so wide,
As John looked down and for a second he froze,
It seemed to change him inside.

Thoughts drifted back of when he was that age,
And the Christmases back in the bay,
Like Scrooge and the Grinch all rolled into one,
His heart grew bigger that day.

The perfect tree they found soon enough,
And made their way back to the house,
But Uncle John wasn't finished there,
Of that there was certainly no doubt.

DON'T BE TALKIN'

He finished the lights and trimmed the tree,
And put Santa and the b'ys on the roof,
He was blocked right full of the Christmas spirit,
Even bought a new tablecloth too.

Then they all sat down for the big Christmas dinner,
John served up the turkey and dressing,
They went 'round the table and one by one,
They all began counting their blessings.

Right after dinner they all gathered 'round,
Feasting on cookies and cake,
The kids were moaning about the car ride back home,
And how long the trip it would take.

Then Suze spoke up, yes, she started again,
Well, why don't you just stay around?
We can go get some fireworks for New Year's Eve,
Or perhaps see the ones out in town.

And we can make some hors d'oeuvres and buy champagne,
Or perhaps you'd rather some wine,
And we can get treats for the youngsters to have,
Right, John? I'm sure you don't mind.

Well, John slumped down in his favourite chair,
And just listened to Aunt Suze's balkin',
You could see him turn red and from under his breath,
He could hear New Year's! Don't be talkin'!

Here's another short story about growing up and spending time with my dad.

Dad's Old Wooden Flat

It's amazing where your mind can take you with one simple picture.

I was looking through an old photo album last week. It's one of those with the padded covers and gold-coloured metal ring bindings. The sheets of plastic that covered each sticky page were falling out. When I first opened it, three or four pictures fell out. One of them really stood out to me. I took a look at it, and I couldn't help but smile.

The picture was of my dad's old wooden flat, taken back when I was about ten or eleven, I suppose. Now, I'm not sure how many of you know what a flat is. Well, if you can picture a dory, with the traditional yellowish-orange dory buff colour and the dark green gunnels, then you're almost there. Take that dory and cut the arse end off of it and board it over. There you have what our family and most others from back home in Placentia Bay would commonly refer to as a flat. The picture was taken in late fall, when the flat was hauled ashore, turned over, and lashed down for the winter.

My mind drifted back to many Saturday mornings. I'll give you an example of what one of those mornings was like. But first, let me fill you in on a couple of things. You see, Dad had a wood stove in the basement. And we were lucky enough to be living across the road from a big pond. The name of the pond is "Big Pond." As you can see, lots of imagination went into the naming. In the summertime, he'd row across the pond, cut down and limb out a pile of wood, load the flat, and row back. But that wasn't all. With each stick on his shoulder, he'd walk up the hill to the house, cut it up with the bucksaw, and store it in the basement.

Winter months, with the pond frozen, he had a wood slide. With the two straps over his shoulder, he'd tow that thing across the pond, cut more wood, load the slide, and tow it back. I don't think there was a tougher or more determined man in Placentia Bay. But I'm getting sidetracked here. Back to the story.

It was usually around eight in the morning when Dad would come into my room and yell out to me. "Come on, get up," he'd say. "We gotta get going! That wood is not going to cut itself." I knew then that my day was planned out. I often tried to come up with some excuse, like I was tired from studying all week, but Dad was having none of it. So, in spite of my alternate plans of going riding on the bikes with my buddies, or taking a walk out around shore for a fire, I gave in to my father and to what I considered at the time to be child labour.

Most every Saturday, I wore the same thing . . . an old pair of rubber boots that were just about worn through the soles, vamps that my grandmother knitted, and Dad's old red-and-black plaid flannel shirt that was thick enough to be a jacket. Then it was time for breakfast, if you could call a quick slice of toast breakfast. Then I headed up to the shed to get the bucksaw and axe for this week's adventures. By this time Dad was already down untying the boat and hauling it in from out on the frape.

In case you don't know what that is, well, it's like an old-time handmade mooring system.

Well, sir, having the flat hauled in is one thing, but being ready to go was quite another. That old flat was as leaky as a basket. Every week it was the same thing. Bail out the boat for a half-hour before we went anywhere. I suggested many times that we chink her up, but I was always met with the same response. "A bit of bailin' never hurt anyone before. Sure, I don't even know where I'd get a bit of oakum, anyway."

Well, once that task was complete, it was time to head across . . . at least Dad did the rowing. In less than fifteen minutes, we'd be on the other side with the flat hauled up in case of high tide. Then, after ten minutes of walking, we were ready to start in. I tell you, that man could cut wood. He was like a one-man wrecking crew . . . well, except for there were two of us. Dad cut them down, and with the small axe that we often referred to as a tomahawk, I limbed them out. It wasn't long after that before we had them loaded aboard the flat. Sticks stuck off in all directions made it look like a floating porcupine to people passing along the road. This was my time to stretch out for a little break. Or so I thought, because by this time, more water leaked in and it was time to start bailing again. You could see a grin on his face as I balanced myself, trying not to fall with each thrust of the oars.

Once back on dry land, we unloaded the sticks and brought them up to the house. Once they were cut up into short twelve-inch junks, my job was to stand on a chair in the basement and take them in through the window and stack them up. I wasn't much of a hand at this, especially with them coming in at lightning speed, as I tried to prevent them from rolling all over the basement floor. Again, Dad appeared to be getting great enjoyment out of watching me struggle.

You'd think that once this was complete our day was done, but oh no. Not when you're working for my dad. Back down to the flat, across the pond once again for a second load, then a third, and maybe even a fourth load if there was enough time before dark.

Many times I complained about how tired I was, or how my arms were hurting. All I'd get from that was a little smirk and, "That'll never hurt ya!"

It's been quite a few years since those days, but those memories will carry with me forever. That picture is framed now and sits on my desk at work. As frustrated and angry as I was at the time, if I could go back to those days, I have to say that I wouldn't change a thing.

Oh, and one more thing . . . thanks, Dad!

How does one elderly lady take down a town's economy? Read on to find out.

Trouble with Tea Buns

Raisin tea buns? I loves 'em, I do,
Especially the ones that are baked by Aunt Suze,
Sure, just last week, I got about four,
For clearing the snow away from her door.

But keep that to yourself, and I'll tell you why,
She had to give them to me on the sly,
See, a few years back, in her infinite wisdom,
Aunt Suze developed a bartering system.

It started real small, between family and friends,
P'raps trade a dozen, for a meal of cod's heads,
There was no one around who could bake them so good,
Once she traded three dozen for two cord of wood.

From a gallon of paint right down to split peas,
She even bartered for whiskey for Uncle John's tea,
She handed them out for work done on her car,
Although you might think that's going too far.

But then Sophie Brown from over in the gut,
Loved the idea, said she wanted a cut,
So Suze passed the recipe, she passed it with pride,
As long as she got her percentage on the side.

Then Soph passed it on to her friend on the hill,
Soon an old lady tea bun network was built,
It wasn't long before the whole town was buzzin',
About the phenomenon of tea buns from Aunt Suze's oven.

They brought them to bake sales, they brought them to wakes,
At the church Suze dropped two in the collection plate,
She used them to get a leak patched in her roof,
And to get the supplies, she paid with buns for that too.

All hands were happy, enjoying the taste,
Eating them up, not a crumb did they waste,
All work got done, and the town it got fed,
There's no better marriage, not even newlyweds.

Now, the whole operation was chugging along,
When they noticed that something was definitely wrong,
Jack's convenience was hurting, things looking rough,
See, no one was buying, they were trading for stuff.

And Timothy's hardware noticed *their* sales were down,
Which brought on a panic all over the town,
Poor Marg closed her bakery, put a sign up "For Rent,"
Couldn't even sell a cookie for not even five cents.

With the town now in shambles, now this wasn't fun,
So they called a town meeting to see what could be done,

DON'T BE TALKIN'

All the problems this caused, they had to discuss,
Aunt Suze apologized, never wanted a fuss.

First was the raisins, they were low on supply,
They even dried all the grapes, so no one could make wine,
The economy was hurting, it was hurting a lot,
Sure, I heard on the news that the dollar had dropped.

But the clinic was busy, said old Dr. Collins,
Because half of the town had cholesterol problems,
Those tea buns were tasty, you can't dispute that,
They were blocked full of taste, but blocked more full of fat.

After little discussion, the decision was made,
The bartering would stop, they'd give up the trade,
Those little old ladies now don't bake a thing,
They said their goodbyes to the bun-baking ring.

Well, it took a while, but now order is restored,
And if you want tea buns, well, you go to the store,
But if late at night when you're out on the go,
You might see Aunt Suze with her knittin' bag in tow.

But don't expect socks or wool hats or mitts,
See, Aunt Suze doesn't have a clue how to knit,
She kept her promise, there's no tea buns at all,
But she's some hand to make chocolate coconut snowballs.

Mary's Crowd

There's a man I know, and my son he's some tight,
You might say he's so tight that he squeaks,
It's Dad's Uncle Bert, he's the best kind of fella,
But I'll tell ya now, b'ys, he's some cheap.

If he could tear a penny in half,
I'll tell ya, he'd be quite contented,
Sure, one time he tried, and now this is fact,
That's how copper wire was invented.

He pins his tea bags out on the line,
He uses them three or four times,
And the same suit of clothes he wears every day,
Since nineteen seventy-nine.

Now Bert's not poor, no, not at all,
In fact, he's worth a bundle,
His mattress is blocked with hundred-dollar notes,
In case of "financial trouble."

He eats real well, has the best kind of grub,
And that's where this story begins,
The mystery is that his pantry is bare,
With neither a bottle nor tin.

So, where does he get all the food that he eats,
When there isn't a morsel around?
Well, you probably won't understand just yet,
But he gets it from "Mary's crowd."

So, I guess that needs a little explaining,
And I assure you these words are not fake,
He looks in the paper when he gets out of bed,
Yes, he looks for the funerals and wakes.

He then dresses up in that old suit of clothes,
The one that I mentioned just now,
Then goes to pay his respects to the corpse,
Saying, "I'm here with Mary's crowd."

Mary's as common a name as you can find,
As common as you could ever believe,
And I bet if you said you were one of that crowd,
You'd never be asked to leave.

The plan worked quite well, he filled up on salads,
And sandwiches made of roast beef,
And raisin tea buns and date squares and cookies,
Washed down with a nice cup of tea.

Now, one such night, he was about to leave,
The keeper was turning out the lights,
To the kitchen he went for a bun for the road,
And a sandwich for later that night.

He said good night from "Mary's crowd,"
With a grin he said, I'm sly as a fox,

But when he came back out, he was all alone,
Except for the one in the box.

He tried for a while to open the door,
But it was locked, he could not find a way,
He wasn't nervous at all to be there,
Sure, the kitchen was like a buffet.

He ate the salads with lettuce and spinach,
And the ones with both mustard and beet,
Blueberry tarts and even Jell-O corn salad,
That stuff that no one would eat.

After a while he was feeling quite full,
Couldn't eat another bite,
He went back in the parlour, lay on the daybed,
He figured he was there for the night.

He had quite the pain in the stomach, you see,
This gluttony had treated him rough,
This surely was a grave mistake,
Shouldn't have eaten that last cream puff.

He started nodding off for a second,
But abruptly he was awakened,
He heard a noise and it got real cold,
He said, Hello? in a voice that was shaking.

My name is Bob, said a ghostly voice,
But most people call me Murph,
And I know who you are, so you don't have to say,
You're the one that they call Bert.

And I know all about your gluttonous ways,
I've seen your face so many times,
I've seen you at every funeral and wake,
And now you're interrupting mine.

Bert couldn't talk, he was frightened to death,
His heart near blowing a gasket,
He slowly glanced at the pine box up front,
"Robert Murphy" written right on the casket.

Murph continued, This path is not right,
You certainly need to make some changes,
If not, he said, it won't be long,
And they'll be making your funeral arrangements.

See, the reason I know you and seen you around,
And I tell you, for this, I'm not proud,
All the food I ate is what got me here,
See, I was with "Agnes's crowd."

Poor Bert didn't know what to do or say,
He felt a bit of remorse,
Perhaps he should quit, yes, give it all up,
And let life take a different course.

Once he made the decision to make the big change,
He felt much more at peace,
He thanked Mr. Murphy and paid his respects,
Before drifting off to sleep.

Around 9:00 a.m. a key turned in the lock,
Bert woke to a bright sunny day,

He made his apologies and thanked everyone there,
And left behind his old ways.

From that day forward his pantry was full,
Wasn't shy of spending a dollar,
But watched what he ate, took care of himself,
Even bought a new suit that was smaller.

He often thought back, Did that really happen?
Or was it that he was just dreaming?
But not wanting to take any chances at all,
He gave up all of his scheming.

Now he still goes and visits the funerals and wakes,
To make things right, he vowed,
He drops off plates of cookies and sandwiches,
With a note that says . . . "From Mary's crowd."

Winter has always been my favourite time of year, until it wasn't.

Winter

The first snowfall is finally here,
It's earlier perhaps than most other years,
The children are happy and shouting with cheer,
What a wonderful time of year.

Now the second snowfall is not far behind,
And to shovel the driveway, I really don't mind,
On lawns of most houses a snowman you'll find,
Yes, wintertime is lovely.

Not long after this we are treated by more,
There's enough to go sledding by this time, I'm sure,
The kids grab their sleds and head for the door,
Oh, the wonderful joys of winter.

With Christmas approaching, I tap on the glass,
Well, it looks like another wintertime blast,
Thirty centimetres more and it's falling real fast,
But I'm sure I'll get through it all right.

Now when this load was finally cleared,
Another pile more was dumped on us here,
With more to follow, the youngsters did cheer,
But now my back is aching.

Then the rain it started for just a bit,
And the temperature dropped to ensure I would slip,
In my driveway on a sheet of this frozen white sh . . . stuff,
This winter is starting to bug me.

Now on the TV and the radio too,
They're saying not to go out unless you got a skidoo,
And stock up on meds for the cold and the flu,
'Cause I think it'll be a hard winter.

Now, Think it'll be, is that what I heard?
I thought that to be just a little absurd?
'Cause we saw that much snow that my vision is blurred,
Oh, the wonderful first half of winter.

Then plow man Bob just over the road,
He'd sit there to wait for another load,
To dump in my driveway every time it did snow,
My nerves are shot from this winter.

I'm sure it's on purpose, no word of a lie,
As he buries me in I sees that big smile,
If he was here now, he'd go down in a pile,
I'll flatten his tires this winter.

Well, that's it for the shovelling, I'll swear on a stack,
I'll pay someone else, yes, that is a fact,

'Cause me shovel is broken, and so is me back,
From all of the snow this winter.

Three times so far, or perhaps it was four,
It froze so hard with winds from the north,
That me pipes they froze up, I had to use a blowtorch,
I'm some frigging sick of this winter.

As the months roll along, the end is in sight,
The waiting is over, yes, I see the light,
I may even shovel out the barbecue tonight,
Oh, I've prayed for the end of this winter.

Next year will be different, I say that each year,
But this time I know it, and that I will swear,
I'll be sitting on a beach sipping on a cold beer,
'Cause I'll be in Florida next winter.

In the summer of 2018, we lost one of the finest people who ever lived, my sister Eva Deir. This short piece is a tribute to this amazing woman. Always loved, never forgotten, forever missed.

The Unfinished Story

On the page was half of a story,
The rest of the words unseen,
Just waiting for the next line,
To come to us like a dream.

But sometimes life is funny,
And some might say unfair,
This story will have no ending,
No final note to share.

Life is but a story,
It was one she wrote quite well,
A kind and gentle soul she was,
As anyone could tell.

HARRY INGRAM

Married at a young age,
Her soulmate soon she found,
Through thick and thin, for better or worse,
They said their wedding vows.

And then the children came along,
A family soon created,
A foundation built on love and trust,
Could not be separated.

The husband strong and proud,
He worked hard every day,
Like his father before him,
Catching fish out in the bay.

Many friendships built in life,
Her kindness had no end,
Not an enemy or acquaintance,
She called everyone a friend.

And oh, the kitchen parties,
Not one soul turned away,
And no matter midnight or 3:00 a.m.,
Lots o' time, she always would say.

With p'raps a boiler of soup on the stove,
Or a turkey in the oven to share,
With guitars and accordions playing along,
We all sang "The Rose in Her Hair."

Many's a time was held such as this,
With not one soul hungry or dry,

And every heart was full as well,
As morning bid farewell to the night.

And then there was the workplace,
She couldn't be outdone,
While working hard day in, day out,
She kept the workplace fun.

Wasn't shy of a joke or story,
To anyone passing by,
Helped everyone laugh and enjoy the day,
She wore the biggest smile.

And then arrived the grandkids,
So precious and so small,
They lit her world like nothing else,
She looked forward to every call.

But the illness came too quickly,
There was so much left to do,
She wasn't ready to say goodbye,
She fought to make it through.

But we watched her fight come to an end,
And all of our hearts, they sank,
Just half of life's story written,
The other half left blank.

We said goodbye to a sister,
A mom, an aunt, and wife,
We said goodbye to an angel,
Who touched everyone in life.

Yes, sometimes life is funny,
And some might say unfair,
This story has no ending,
No final note to share.

Life is but a story,
It was one she wrote quite well,
A kind and gentle soul she was,
Loves ya, sis . . . farewell.

The Remote

Walk in any home and I'm sure that you'll find,
A thing full of buttons, about two inches by five,
They come in all colours, and some even glow,
A handy little thing, it's called the remote.

You can get them for anything now, I'm sure,
From TVs to stereos, ceiling fans, and more,
From little toy boats to Christmas yule logs,
My daughter even got a remote puppy dog.

When the family dog got a load of that,
Well, he barked and yelped, you'd think it was a cat,
He flicked at it and pawed at it and wanted to chew,
So, I engaged the shock collar, there's a remote for that too.

I can't wait 'til they invent one for the fridge,
Imagine that, now, oh what would it bring,
One button to open, another to close,
And bring me a can of cold beer, I suppose.

I've searched twenty minutes, and often times thirty,
And missed half my show with panic and worry,
For the TV remote, both up and downstairs,
Only to find the damned thing wedged down in the chair.

How foolish is that? the wife often mocked me,
You're looking under the couch instead of at hockey,
Why don't you just walk over instead,
And push the little button, oh, where is your head?

You spend half your time with them silly old things,
When the garden needs work, and it has since the spring.
So my mission in life now, even though it sounds shocking,
Is to find a remote that will make her stop talking.

So, to count them all up, now, I don't mean to boast,
I'd say I have almost a dozen remotes,
Upstairs there are three, and downstairs there are seven,
And the one in the bedroom, sure, that makes eleven.

Now, when I was a boy, there wasn't one seen,
You turned a big dial to watch the TV,
Things sure did change from those days long ago,
When I think of it now, *I* was the remote.

Go change the channel, my father would say,
Turn on the news, anything happen today?
CBC, NTV, and then back again,
All those trips to the TV, I made way back when.

Well, this ends the tribute to the remote control,
And the batteries that come with it, too, I suppose,
So I'll keep an eye to the flyers, and on eBay I'll bid,
In hopes they'll invent a remote for the kids.

Up in Smoke

You have the right to remain silent! and phrases like that,
Are things I don't want to hear,
No, I never wish to stand before,
A jury of my peers.

Some crimes can be quite serious,
And land you in the slammer,
But some can be plain foolish,
Yes, here's one quick example.

The police station, it got robbed,
But only the toilets were stolen,
And after the search for leads concluded,
They still have nothing to go on.

Not all examples are as foolish as this,
In fact, they can be quite clever,
So, here's a little story I heard,
Let's see if I remember.

This story concerns a lawyer,
And if you committed a crime,
There's no one in the world,
You'd rather standing at your side.

He knew all the ins and outs there were,
Put criminals on the shelf,
And in the case that lies before us,
He even represented himself.

He bought himself some fine cigars,
For what's next you'll think I'm a liar,
He took out an insurance policy,
Against everything, including . . . fire.

He then sat down and smoked them all,
Lit each one with its own little flame,
And when this box of Cubans was gone,
He decided to open his claim.

But the insurance company wouldn't pay,
They said, My son, you're mad,
But his I's were dotted and T's were crossed,
His case was ironclad.

Twenty-four thousand, they were forced to pay,
In spite of their lack of desire,
He proved beyond the shadow of a doubt,
His property was destroyed by fire.

In court, the judge was disgusted,
But had to rule for the plaintiff,
He said, Get this man out of my court,
And gestured to the bailiff.

That's a fine story, you might think to yourself,
But the story is only half-told,

DON'T BE TALKIN'

The insurance company was poisoned,
And opened a case of their own.

They used the lawyer's testimony,
The one from the previous case,
They used his words against him,
And the lawyer met his fate.

Twenty-four cases of arson,
The judge proceeded to tell,
Two thousand dollars for each one,
The judge's gavel fell.

The lawyer was found guilty,
As the judge read his decision,
He said, You've brought this on yourself,
Guilty by your own admission.

From here he had nowhere to go,
His reputation was ruined,
The life sucked out of his practice,
Deflated like a balloon.

For income, well, he tried real hard,
To win the weekly lotto,
But ended up behind a desk,
Selling insurance, home and auto.

A talking moose. That's really all that needs to be said about this one.

Jerome

Now, Old Skipper Bill hove off his chair,
Listening to the stories and lies,
The young fellas talked about poaching moose,
And jigging a few fish on the sly.

Each story told was more far-fetched,
Than the one told before,
Skipper Bill had enough, and said,
Listen now, b'ys, I've got a fine tale in store.

'Twas the early '70s, or was it my early seventies?
I really can't remember that far,
When I took me boat and went out on the pond,
I figured I'd stay there 'til dark.

With me old bamboo pole and me tub o' worms,
I ventured a good ways off shore,
It was just a small flat with no motor at all,
With thole-pins in the gunnels and oars.

HARRY INGRAM

Well, a half-dozen trout was all that I caught,
But I really could not have cared less,
With the water so calm and the sun on my face,
It seemed a good time to rest.

Just the sound of the birds in that crisp morning air,
And a gentle wind rustling the trees,
With the full day ahead to finish my catch,
I began to drift off to sleep.

Then all of a sudden, a gunshot blast!
Sure, I nearly jumped out of my skin,
And two more followed right after,
And a voice yelling, Shoot 'im ag'in!

Then out of the woods like the shot from the gun,
Came a moose looking around for protection,
He looked all around, looked up and then down,
Like a CFA looking for directions.

Well, the thought crossed my mind to grab the oars,
And head to the other side,
But as I looked all around, I soon realized,
They were carried away with the tide.

Well, the moose left the shore and swam out to me,
And here I had nowhere to go,
And what his intentions were with me,
I didn't think I wanted to know.

It wasn't what I expected at all,
As I stared in the face of this moose,

DON'T BE TALKIN'

He seemed to say, Buddy, I need some help,
And I said, Yes buddy, me too.

He then with his rack took the painter in tow,
And dragged me safe to the shore,
I said, B'y, you just saved my skin,
So I guess it's now time to save yours.

So, I knew a shortcut back to the truck,
As the moose followed close behind,
When we got there, I motioned to the pan of the truck,
And pretty soon, in it he climbed.

Lid down flat just like he was dead,
Sprawled off in the pan of me truck,
Passing by hunters with their guns and their vests,
Quite jealous of my fortune and luck.

Well, back to my home we arrived soon enough,
And I pulled 'round the back out of house,
As soon as he seen we were all alone,
He quickly hopped up and got out.

That was a close one, this moose says to me,
That was just before I passed out,
Then coming to, to see it wasn't a dream,
I was gone for another round.

I finally woke up and came to grips,
Then started to regain my composure,
I thanked him and said, Now be on your way,
He said, Humph, not until moose season's over.

To argue with a beast of this monstrous size,
I didn't even bother to try,
I just cleared a spot in the back of the shed,
I said now that should do for the night.

Then what a commotion about quarter to three,
That brought me right to my feet,
I went downstairs and looked out on the deck,
At this moose covered up in a sheet.

And not just a sheet he had wrapped 'round his head,
And tangled all up in his points,
'Twas the clothesline and all with wool socks, pants, and bras,
All snarled up with patio lights.

He lowered his head and apologized to me,
He said, Would you mind if I came in the house?
It's awful lonely out there in the shed,
I promise I'll be quiet as a mouse.

I let him squeeze in, p'raps a stunned thing to do,
It's a good thing we got double doors,
He wasn't stood up for a second and a half,
Before sprawling on the hardwood floor.

He looked a bit like Bambi on steroids,
The way Bambi sprawled off on the ice,
He finally got up on the daybed,
With the daybed now nowhere in sight.

Next morning he was hungry and I didn't know,
What I should give him to eat,

He didn't like bottles of sweet mustard pickles,
Nor did he like bottles of beet.

So, moose are vegetarians, you see,
So, my bottles of meat were no use,
I couldn't offer bottled rabbit or turr,
And, heaven forbid, bottled moose.

With his hoof he pointed out to the backyard,
He said, Here's a deal for you, Skipper,
You won't need to mow it as long as I'm here,
Just don't try to feed me them flippers.

With his diet all sorted and lodging somewhat,
For work I tried not to be late,
Then break time I stopped to check the news,
There's a moose in Quidi Vidi Lake!

It wasn't long before I arrived on the scene,
With the Wildlife Officer there too,
I said, Buddy, he's only gettin' a drink,
Not like he's in the McDonald's drive-thru.

Then after a while we started agreeing,
And we figured out what would be best,
He was no longer allowed out parading around town,
Without a huge orange vest.

So there you have it, he stayed for a while,
And everything worked out just fine,
He ate all the grass out in our backyard,
And his antlers we used for clotheslines.

He went back in the woods when the hunters came out,
But don't think that it all ends here,
He's become a good friend of the family,
And visits us every year.

Now, the young fellas couldn't believe it at all,
They thought he was drinking the juice,
There was no way in the world that this could be true,
I mean, really, a talking moose?

Bill just smiled and looked at his watch,
Said, I think that it's time I head home,
For the last ten minutes my ride's been outside,
It's a big bull moose named Jerome.

You've heard of a Furby? Or perhaps a Hatchimal?
Well, allow me to introduce . . .

Whatchamabot

What's new this year, I can't say that I know,
But the youngsters can tell ya, sure they got me drove,
Each year before Christmas, they comb catalogues,
And they're all over Wish, eBay, and Amazon.

So, you heard of the Furby, or p'raps Hatchimals,
They're little talking robots, do anything at all,
But there's one new contraption, outshines the whole lot,
Most intelligent yet, called the Whatchamabot.

You can teach it to speak eight languages in total,
And dance and sing, even teach it to yodel,
It can read you the news, or jokes just for fun,
It's like Alexa and Siri all rolled into one.

The most blatant of hints helped us figure out,
Just what to get them, online with no crowds,
I tried Amazon, it said February first,
For the next load of stock, oh my, that's the worst.

Then we tried the other two, eBay and Wish,
But in the swimming pool, I'd have more luck jiggin' a fish,
So the traditional way, it seems quite ambitious,
Out facing the crowds two weeks before Christmas.

So we strolled into Walmart the very next day,
Not one of them left, sir, I'm sorry to say,
But we'll have more in on December nineteenth,
But you'd better come early, it'll be quite the scene.

So we furthered our search, oh my, what a fuss,
Even tried Canadian Tire, and of course Toys R Us,
Every store in the mall, yes, we tried the whole lot,
But still no sign of that Watchamabot.

The time it passed by, yes, the day it arrived,
We got up and got ready at quarter past five,
The first ones there was our goal in mind,
But were half a mile away at the back of the line.

Then all of a sudden, those big glass doors opened,
And anything not nailed down was trampled or broken,
One fella named Frank looking for poinsettia flowers,
Got caught in the throng, lost his wife for three hours.

When me and the wife finally reached the display,
There was only one left, this was our lucky day,
So she went to grab it, we were all full of smiles,
When another set of hands reached out at the same time.

It was quite the standoff, just like the old west,
I wasn't much help, I have to confess,

As they squared off together, I heard my wife say,
In a gravelly voice, Go ahead, make my day.

A crowd soon gathered to see who'd be the victor,
But the wife too slow, yes, she should have been quicker,
You see, while they shot daggers into each other's eyes,
A third set of hands grabbed a hold of the prize.

So we headed back home, not much else we could do,
With the Whatchamabot shortage all over the news,
We were deep in despair, no other options, really,
When a light bulb came on, the wife shouted, Kijiji!

Why didn't we think about checking there before,
Instead of wasting our time with the lineups and stores?
And sure enough, there were three there for sale,
But that price tag? My son, they should be in jail.

So, we messaged and asked to drop by for a look,
He seemed pretty sketchy, possibly a crook,
Now, I've never done drugs or been part of a deal,
But I'm willing to bet that's how it would feel.

So, he picked a location for where we should meet,
The old Costco parking lot, yes, nice and discreet,
As he whispered the price from under his breath,
He was looking around like someone frightened to death.

He passed me the toy and then grabbed the cash,
And just like that, sir, he was gone like the flash,
I wondered to myself what the hurry was for,
And just then I saw them, two dozen or more.

Parents were running, some with youngsters in tow,
Heading straight for us, so quickly we drove,
Yes, we drove away avoiding this horde,
As fast as we could, with this . . . thing aboard.

We got home and hid it for the kids not to find,
In a couple of days they'll go out of their minds,
I was so very pleased with what we had got,
We were finally the owners of a Whatchamabot.

Well, I guess the next step was to just take it easy,
We checked our list, it was done completely,
With Christmas so close, we had two days to spare,
Decorations up and the baking prepared.

Then one of our children came into the room,
Jumping up and down, almost over the moon,
Pointing at the flyer, hardly able to talk,
Mommy and Daddy, this is what I want.

But that Whatchamabot you've been dying to get,
As my thoughts progressed, I broke into a sweat,
Oh, none of my friends like those things anymore,
And besides, there's none of them left at the store.

I looked at my watch and then at my missus,
Picked up the flyer and thought *Merry Christmas*,
Let's get going, sure, time we got lots,
I just hope this isn't another Whatchamabot.

This piece was written after a visit with my sister and brother-in-law. This is based loosely on a true story about his grandfather, "Old Mr. Frank."

The Long Road

Through his torn denim jacket,
The winter wind blew,
As he stood on the highway,
In his old worn-out shoes.

Trying to shelter from,
The snow mixed with rain,
With another set of headlights,
Passing by him again.

Then stopping beside him,
A big cargo van,
Where ya headed, my son,
He said, Newfoundland.

My name's Jim,
Said the man at the wheel,

HARRY INGRAM

Hop on in, boy,
I'll make you a deal.

The young man said, Michael,
As Jim's hand he shook,
He climbed aboard,
And the deal he took.

The deal that Jim offered,
Was to bring him back home,
In exchange for the company,
On that long lonely road.

So, what's your story?
He asked the young man,
Mike just leaned over,
With his head in his hands.

I spent half my life,
And money on the streets,
With the things that I purchased,
You can't get receipts.

I turned on my family,
For a life full of crime,
To pay for my habits,
Now I don't have a dime.

How long you been away?
'Bout ten years or so,
And if my family will want me,
I don't really know.

DON'T BE TALKIN'

I had to move home,
He said with a frown,
Yes, I need a change,
Turn my whole life around.

I spent six weeks in rehab,
And I have to admit,
It felt like forever,
But taught me quite a bit.

They talked for a while,
And slept in between,
They talked of their travels,
And the sights that they've seen.

Then finally the ferry,
It came into view,
The trip will soon end,
And I'll start life anew.

The driver and traveller,
Now both parted ways,
Wished each other the best,
In their upcoming days.

It was not what he expected,
As he reached his hometown,
His family, they shunned him,
He felt so beat down.

With both parents passed,
On his brother's door he knocked,

And his sister's as well,
But they kept their doors locked.

He had nowhere to turn,
Not a cent in the bank,
It was just then he thought,
About old Mr. Frank.

He had a rough exterior,
But a kind, gentle soul,
Mike spent much of his youth,
With Frank down in the cove.

A wet and cold night,
He tapped on his door,
It was just like he saw him,
Not two days before.

Old Mr. Frank,
Over his glasses he peered,
Mike, you're not much to look at,
Why don't you shave off that beard?

You're satched to the skin,
Come on in, my son,
And here's some dry clothes,
Now go put them on.

Frank took the wet clothes,
Pinned them up on the line,
That hung just above,
The wood stove to dry.

DON'T BE TALKIN'

Mike told his story,
They talked to no end,
And he thanked Mr. Frank,
For being a friend.

But your time has not come,
Said Frank from the heart,
Anyone can change,
You just need a fresh start.

The next day was brighter,
A new day had dawned,
Frank knew the right guy,
Who could get him a job.

So down at the mill,
He worked day and night,
So very determined,
To make all things right.

The evenings he spent,
With old Mr. Frank,
Cutting down trees,
Turning them into planks.

He taught him to hunt,
Yes, he taught him a lot,
He taught him to cook,
All the food that he caught.

And where to pick berries,
And how to make jam,

And how to save money,
By living off the land.

It wasn't too long,
'Fore a house, it was built,
With the planks from the wood,
That they cut on the hill.

Mike grew as a man,
His mind was strong too,
Mr. Frank had taught him,
All that he knew.

He found a good wife,
With a child on the way,
For all he received,
He could never repay.

But a corner of emptiness,
Was left in his heart,
He reached out to his family,
Asked for a fresh start.

With all that he'd proven,
His old life in the past,
They welcomed him back,
It was all he could ask.

Not two years ago,
He needed a change,
And here he is now,
With his life rearranged.

DON'T BE TALKIN'

With things in perspective,
And a future so bright,
His debts all repaid,
He set all things right.

As the years, they passed by,
Old Frank met his end,
His health, it had failed,
And Mike said goodbye to his friend.

Mike shed a tear,
But for him he gave thanks,
Yes, he owed his whole life,
To old Mr. Frank.

My teen years were quite adventurous living in a small town. Quite often we'd head "out around shore" for a fire. Of course, some of the content of this story is exaggerated, and there are certainly some truths as well. This one is for the b'ys!

Arson Around

So, what do you do when you live 'round the bay,
    On days and nights that you're bored?
   I know a few things you just might do,
    I was there, if the truth be told.

Now, I don't mean last week or last month,
    Those days are well in the past,
But when I was young, way back in the day,
    Imaginations could not be surpassed.

With nothing to do on a fine Saturday,
    As we stabbed jellyfish on the beach,
We had a discussion, sure, it can't be that hard,
    A world record can't be far out of reach.

So, next was the challenge of figuring out,
What record we'd try to break,
Ches said he'd eat the most hot wings,
And Dave, the biggest steak.

Then Jim spoke up from out in the kitchen,
But what he said, sure, I couldn't make out,
So I turned to look, and there he stood,
Six capelin stogged in his mouth.

We're not going to see how many of those,
You can fit in your gob at one time,
And anyway, sure, that's not near enough,
I think the record is twenty-nine.

So, after researching some of the oddest,
World records you could ever imagine,
We finally decided and all agreed,
It was time to make this happen.

I believe it was Norway that held the record,
For the tallest bonfire to date,
I think they said it was forty-five metres,
In feet that's one forty-eight.

We thought that was nothing, sure, just last week,
In a big forty-five-gallon drum,
Dad was out back burning garbage,
And I'll tell ya, b'ys, that was some hum.

He was burning everything that you could imagine,
You'd probably go to jail for it now,

With the flames shooting up fifty feet in the air,
And, sure, that was when it died down.

So, we picked the location, 'twas out around shore,
See, we're kind of smart like that,
Right close to the water, just in case,
The fire would get out of hand.

We recruited more fellas, there was Mike and Steve,
Dwayne, and I think there was Ted,
We gathered up tires and wood from the beach,
And some gas that we stole from Jim's shed.

We got all set up and called the crowd,
That verifies world record placements,
We were all excited to beat the Norwegians,
Except Jim, he was still eating capelin.

Put them down and lets get 'er done,
We still have work left to do,
We headed out, me and the b'ys,
And the world record camera crew.

We started it small just down from a cliff,
Sure, we went out the day before,
To mark all the heights on the face of that rock,
How we're still living, I'm not really sure.

So, after the fire started to grow,
We threw in an old lobster pot,
Then a couple of pallets and half a tree,
And if you think that's a lot . . .

There were seventeen tires, an old wooden dresser,
We burned the drawers one at a time,
A table and chairs set and a small wooden boat,
We found on the beach past her prime.

The flames got higher, we were getting close,
But the goal, we couldn't get past,
So Dwayne climbed up on top of the cliff,
He was holding the can of gas.

I bawled out to everyone to get out of the way,
As I tossed in an old wooden graplin,
But Jim didn't hear, he was all distracted,
He was busy roasting his capelin.

Then from up on top Dwayne poured the gas,
For to get this record we vowed,
He thought at this point there was nothing to lose,
Well, except perhaps his eyebrows.

It was all we could do, not a thing left to burn,
But the record we just couldn't win,
All the work we had put into this,
We all felt kind of grim.

Then the lady from the record books,
Said, There's no reason to be blue,
You might not have reached your ultimate goal,
But I've got a question for you.

We've been keeping a close eye on your bonfire,
And I'm pretty impressed, I must say,

But how many capelin has that young man eaten,
Since the beginning of the day?

We all had a laugh and said that's just Jim,
I'd say he had nearly five dozen,
But it's the same thing almost every day,
Maybe barbecued or done in the oven.

Well, after discussing and calculating,
Everything worked out just fine,
'Cause Jim won the record for one single day,
The most capelin consumed at one time.

We were all ecstatic, about to burst,
We couldn't hardly believe,
The goal we set a few days before,
In a way, I guess, we achieved.

So, I guess if you want something bad enough,
It may not be far out of reach,
Just remember Jim, the world record holder,
And that memorable day on the beach.

Dog Harbour Treasure

Pirates, I said, in Placentia Bay?
I don't believe it, there's certainly no way,
But Uncle Mose vowed as the tale he began,
I'll tell you about Dizzy, oh, his real name is Sam.

They called him Dizzy, there's a reason for that,
Out on the water, well, he just couldn't stand,
Now, I certainly don't mean he didn't like it at all,
He just couldn't stand up, when he tried, he would fall.

To make a living, the fishery was no good,
So he went to St. John's and stuck his nose in the books,
And when he came back he was smart as a top,
He knew just about everything, 'cause he studied the lot.

But one of his passions, he learned all about,
Was the Dog Harbour treasure, and he had to find out,
It was on a full moon, with everything silent,
In the late 1800s, put there by pirates.

He could be a carpenter, but that wasn't his thing,
Or go into politics, throw his hat in the ring,
Or start building boats, he could work at his leisure,
But all he wanted, was that Dog Harbour treasure.

There were all sorts of rumours from people who've tried,
Who saw headless pirates, took heart attacks and died,
But he was convinced, none of this to be true,
For Dog Harbour he left, just him, with no crew.

He walked 'round the harbour, it was quite a long haul,
With safety boots and shovel until nearly nightfall,
A boat would save time, three hours, I 'lows,
But he'd definitely fall overboard and most likely drown.

Oh yes, one more thing, he had slung on his back,
A metal detector, he'd certainly need that,
He reached the harbour and stood high on a rock,
To get his bearings, where X marks the spot.

According to the map as he sized up the chart,
It seemed really close, he was right on the mark,
So to prove all he'd calculated was correct,
He used the metal detector to have a quick check.

Well, sure enough, that needle went wild,
He was all overcome, he was just like the child,
It didn't take long 'fore he started to dig,
And every now and then he'd stop for a swig.

Oh yes, he brought rum, I forgot to inform,
In case he got cold, that'd sure keep him warm,
He was down two feet when stopped for a spell,
And he was down two inches on his bottle as well.

Then all of a sudden the air got real cold,
He got a bit of a fright, if the truth it were told,

DON'T BE TALKIN'

Then a voice he heard that sounded bizarre,
It wasn't even a word, it just sounded like, Yarr.

So ye wants me treasure, said the man who appeared,
He was all dressed in black, said his name was Blackbeard,
In 1887 we buried that gold,
Dizzy said, Yes b'y! you must be some old.

What happened to your hand, there's a hook in its place,
And what's up with the patch you got stuck on your face?
Blackbeard was struck stunned, bare knew what to say,
As Dizzy kept digging, now three feet in clay.

I fought with a crocodile back in no man's land,
I took his life, but he got me hand,
And as for the eye patch, me own eye I took,
One day it was itchy . . . first day with the hook.

Dizzy started to laugh, he laughed 'til he cried,
But Blackbeard was frustrated, You should be petrified,
Not laughing and joking, I'm a pirate, he said,
I could cut off your arm or even your head.

But Dizzy kept digging, with no time to dawdle,
After taking another drop from his bottle,
I'm real glad to meet you, and where are you from?
Oh, where are me manners? Dizzy passed him the rum.

And make yourself useful and pass that device,
That metal detector, can you do anything right?
Another quick try told him all that he needed,
Still dead on the mark, as Dizzy proceeded.

Blackbeard was furious, he said, I'll have your life,
B'y, if you take me, you'll have to tackle the wife,
That's not something you wants, I can guarantee that,
She's fought everything from bull moose to cats.

I guess all the bravery came from the rum,
He wasn't thinking 'bout pirates or possible outcomes,
But Blackbeard had enough, he said, I guarantee,
You won't get me treasure, no, you won't succeed.

He took Dizzy's shovel and even his boots,
He blew out his lantern and drank his rum too,
Then Blackbeard was gone in one puff of smoke,
Dizzy must have passed out, 'cause he didn't see him go.

He woke in the morning with the sun in his eyes,
Had a bit of a headache, there's not much wonder why,
All of it seemed a bit hazy, all right,
As he tried to recall what had happened last night.

Was there really a pirate? He didn't really know,
He gathered his gear and decided to go,
He tried one last time, the ground under his feet,
No metal detected, now how could this be?

Then Uncle Mose stopped and he started to laugh,
You can't stop the story and only tell half,
Oh no, he said, I'll continue on,
And explain to you where the treasure was gone.

See, I met up with Dizzy in the upcoming days,
He explained to me how his mind was a haze,

And there wasn't really a treasure at all,
Or even a pirate, see, the rum did it all.

But if you're wondering at all why the machine it measured,
And the needle was moving and showed Dizzy the treasure,
The next day he realized it wasn't the loot,
But the metal detector found steel toes in his boots.

So, that's it for Dizzy, he's not searching no more,
He wouldn't hardly pick up a dime off the floor,
He might try for a trout or a salmon for pleasure,
But he's staying away from pirates,
And that Dog Harbour treasure.

C Is for Christmas

C is for Christmas, I know it is near,
I hope you enjoy our concert this year,
The joy of the season filled up their hearts,
As they watched me up there, I was saying my part.

Yes, proud of me, I knew they'd be,
So, I waved to my parents, all filled with glee,
What little stars we were that night,
Trying our best to get each part right.

As the concert came to a close,
Not a dry eye was there, in ne'er seat nor row,
Oh what fun to reflect on those days,
The days that I'll cherish in so many ways.

Now let us fast forward about ten years or so,
A teenager then with a lifetime to go,
Christmas seemed a little different somehow,
Without the concerts or big smiling crowds.

But the spirit of Christmas still filled the air,
Just the times they changed from year to year,
With presents to buy for my nephews and nieces,
There was just Mom and Dad, now the list it increases.

Through all the teen years I stayed full of cheer,
Mummered a bit and drank a few beer,
Spending time with family and many good friends,
Is the teenagers' Christmas, I remember it well.

Now here we are, a little later in life,
I've grown up a little and found me a wife,
With beautiful children that I hold so dear,
And a new-found love for Christmas each year.

When babies they were, just starting to grow,
Their minds would be captured by the lights all aglow,
And all of the presents that Santa had brought,
In Christmas pyjamas, they played with the lot.

Yes, they played with all of the gifts they received,
With more wrapping paper than you could ever believe,
How simple life was for children that age,
As this story of Christmas has written a new page.

So, as life rolls along I find myself there,
Sitting and waiting in those hard plastic chairs,
The mumbles of chatter among the whole crowd,
As anticipation builds, I was never so proud.

I watched the whole thing with a lump in my throat,
As she said her part as I did long ago,
Yes, C is for Christmas, I know it is near,
Oh, how I enjoyed the concert this year.

Bert's Not Well

You hear about what happened to Bert? Whadda ya mean? Bert who?

Bert, b'y! 'E's married to me Aunt Mildred, or Aunt Millie, I mean. Dass what everybody calls her. Now, Bert's real name is Lloyd, but there were already two Lloyds in the community, and when you only got 136 people, and two of 'em were named Lloyd, well, you can't really afford another one. Imagine the confusion. So, Lloyd Albert Upshall became Bert.

And why isn't he Uncle Bert? I mean, he's not me uncle. Aunt Millie is not me real aunt either, but for as long as I can remember, everybody called her Aunt Millie. I even asked why one time, and all I got out of that question was an answer that only raised more questions. 'Cause that's the way it was. Okay, well thanks for explaining that. But we're not here to talk about me relations. We're here to talk about how sick Bert got last fall. Some thought his heart give out. Others thought he just had the old hag for a spell. But no sir, nothing like that could do the job on Bert like this did.

Bert was one of the toughest fellas I ever saw. Arms the size around as beef buckets, a chest like that big wrestler fella on the Bugs Bunny cartoons, and legs the size of tree trunks. And the paws on 'im! My son, all his fingers were like long thumbs, and 'is thumbs were like long big toes. Giant of a man.

There was one young fella tried to get after 'is sister one time. Well, he just turned red and said he was going to have a little "talk" with him. Poor young fella, never seen 'im after. Luh, here I go, gettin' away from the story again.

Bert was down to the Legion for a game of darts. He was after havin' a few beer, p'raps a few dozen, who knows? No one ever seen 'im drunk. But he must've been awful warm. The sweat started pourin' off 'im. Then all of a sudden, down 'e went, sir, just like that juniper we cut down on back o' the house two years ago. B'y, we got some wood out of that. Kept the wood stove going for handy two winters.

Anyway, back to Bert. Aunt Millie thought that all the booze finally caught up to him. So, she got her brother Cec to come down on his quad with the big trailer he got on 'er for haulin' out his moose every year. Now, I figure he's at that all the time. I was over to his place, and he got two deep-freezes chocked right full of sausages, roasts, and steaks. You name it, he got it, not to mention what 'e's after givin' away. But, sure I s'pose dass 'is own business, 'ey b'y.

So, Cec and the b'ys dragged Bert outside and got 'im on the trailer, and Aunt Millie managed somehow to get 'im in the house and into the bed. Next morning he seemed all right again, but Aunt Millie wasn't pleased at all. I thought she was gonna haul the head off 'im. See, she used to smoke an awful lot, three or four packs a day, I figures, 'til the doctor told her she had to knock off or she'd end up with something. Don't remember what it was. Begins with an E. Empha... something. She's on the patch now, but if she can't get on any better than that, I'm bringing 'er up a couple of packs 'til she learns how to ca'm down a bit.

Well, Bert was fine for a few days until the same thing happened. This time it was out in the boat. B'ys had the devil of a time trying to get him in out of that. And this time he didn't even have a drop. That got all hands thinkin' the worst. I figured they all had 'im give up for dead. Sure, young Jimmy Dicks was talkin' about making a big box to put 'im in because he wouldn't fit in a casket.

Anyway, the next day he still wasn't feelin' the greatest, so he went to see the doctor. Now, we only got a small clinic here, and it's only opened on Tuesdays and Thursdays from 2:00 to 4:30. That's on account of Dr. Hammond servicing eight communities and making house calls besides. B'y, I don't know how 'is wife puts up with 'im bein' gone all the time like that.

The doctor did a whole bunch of tests on 'im and said 'e'd have the results in two weeks. Well, after about a week and a half, I figured 'twas about as well to bring a hearse instead of the results. What a state 'e was in.

'E finally went back to the doctor and got the results. Seems he was in perfect health, but the doctor said he needed to cut down on the smoking. Now, I've known Bert since I was born, and sure enough, there was a good many bottles up to 'is lips, all right, but never did I see a cigarette.

Doctor said it was way too strong of a patch 'e was wearin'. B'y, Bert was just struck stunned. 'E wouldn't have even known what a patch was except fer Aunt Millie. Anyway, Doc Hammond ca'med him down, and they all figured out what was goin' on. Seems that when Aunt Millie and Bert were in the bed, she rolled over and her patch came off. Then Bert rolled over onto her patch and was wearing it for a spell.

Sure, make no wonder 'e was sick. Just like 'e was smokin' three packs a day. Well, they finally got 'im staightened out, and I s'pose everything is all right now. I saw 'im down to the

Legion last week. He was doing some talking about everything and everyone. Doc Hammond this, Aunt Millie that. Sure, drop down to the house later on for a yarn. I heard just about everything he was sayin'.

Poor Aunt Millie, b'y. Havin' to put up with someone gossipin' all the time like that.

Some Assembly Required

Isn't it great when the larger gifts,
Are the ones that Santa Claus brings,
When they're already put together for you,
And you don't have to do a thing.

But moms and dads around the world,
I'll certainly say I've admired,
Mostly because of three little words,
"Some assembly required."

And then becoming a parent myself,
It certainly rang out clear,
I've done my share of construction as well,
In the passing of the years.

Those blessed Christmas mornings,
The screams of glee so nice,
But Mommy, why are Daddy's hands bandaged?
And why are they packed with ice?

Now, it wasn't nearly half as bad,
Back when the kids were small,
Most all their toys were in one piece,
A stuffed animal, a book, or a ball.

And then there came these high-class gadgets,
The ones with the buzzers and bells,
Said to improve your youngsters' IQ,
"Pediatrician approved" as well.

But the babies would have none of this,
This education-improving device,
They'd much rather play with the box it came in,
Like the cats would play with mice.

And then they get a little older,
With sentences starting to form,
Old enough to want to help,
But on the subject? Not very informed.

Sweetheart, can you please pass the wrench?
As I gave her a kiss on the nose,
This, Daddy? she asked, as I turned to look,
No, sweetie, that's the garden hose.

It's the long metal thing with the rubber on the handle,
Can you please pass it to me?
Never mind, honey, just go get your mother,
I'm pinned under this trampoline.

But that was then and this is now,
As they reach their teenage years,
Most gifts now will fit in your pocket,
And I don't end up in tears.

Well, not from hard labour anyway,
And in case you think I'm jokin',

DON'T BE TALKIN'

My wallet is empty and credit cards maxed,
It's a different kind of broken.

But it's better than the alternative,
As I reflect back once more,
Those late nights that we stayed awake,
Until 3:00 a.m. or four.

Drinking two litres of Diet Pepsi,
And coffee to keep us awake,
So tired of all the slots A and slots B,
Not sure how much more we could take.

And those little tiny screwdrivers you'd get,
Not much bigger than a toothpick in size,
You'd want the hand of a surgeon,
For this tedious exercise.

And then on Christmas morning,
After twenty-five minutes of sleep,
Children yelling about the mountains of toys,
Ears piercing with every scream.

Oh, the wonderful things we got from Santa,
Come on, Mom and Dad, wake up!
But why did Santa bring Pepsi bottles,
And half-empty coffee cups?

But I do miss those times with tiny arms,
Around your neck so tight,
With loving hugs and kisses,
Setting everything just right.

HARRY INGRAM

I miss the sounds of little feet,
Creeping down the stairs,
And how it warms your heart so much,
Without any worries or cares.

What I don't miss are all the headaches,
And the late nights being so tired,
And still cringe whenever I hear those words,
"Some assembly required."

But bruises and scrapes will disappear,
So everyone remember,
Those wonderful Christmas memories,
Are sure to last forever.

Many songs, stories, and parodies have been written about COVID-19. Here's my take on the pandemic. There will be an end.

The Other End of This

On the other end of this,
I s'pose 'twill be a brighter day,
On the other end of this,
Sure, all the kids can go and play.

They can visit Grandma,
Give her a hug and kiss,
It'll be a much more happy time,
On the other end of this.

We won't have to stay indoors,
On the other end of this,
And within a six-foot square together,
We will coexist.

We will comfort loved ones,
In case they feel downtrodden,

On the other end of this,
Sure, all will be forgotten.

We can go and share a brew,
On the other end of this,
The first round will be on me,
And that I will insist.

And when the band does grace the stage,
You can ask someone to dance,
No more swiping right on Tinder,
To start a new romance.

The family will go out to dine,
On the other end of this,
We'll have steak or pork back ribs,
Or maybe deep-fried fish,

Or maybe just a salad,
That would probably be more wise,
'Cause since this whole thing started,
We've been baking cakes and pies.

On the other end of this,
Sure, we can go and see a show,
Dance recitals, concerts,
Spending time with folks we know.

The kids will be excited,
Getting back to friends they've missed,
There'll be high-fives and hugs galore,
On the other end of this.

DON'T BE TALKIN'

Speaking of the children,
They'll all head back to school,
Learning will commence once more,
As they follow all the rules.

Some will be delighted,
And think of this as bliss,
But parents will be happiest,
On the other end of this.

If we catch a cold or flu,
On the other end of this,
We'll get a box of tissues,
And some meds that can assist,

Or maybe visit a doctor,
If the symptoms don't subside,
And sneeze into our elbow,
Without being terrified.

Mother Nature will be happy,
On the other side of this,
We're helping the earth recover,
That's a fact you can't dismiss.

The world is slowing down,
There's less pollution in the air,
On the other side of this,
I hope we'll all be more aware.

So, as I wait for this to end,
I have to stop and think,

HARRY INGRAM

With everything all cleaned and polished,
Including the kitchen sink.

Time spent as a family,
Sure, that won't make you sad,
With baking nights and craft nights,
And board games aren't so bad.

So, in the meantime, we'll eat well,
While spending precious time,
And know that on the other end,
It all will work out fine.

We'll have a cup of tea online,
And yarn with all we miss,
And, my son, there'll be some party,
On the other end of this.

Acknowledgements

If having friends is a measure of wealth, then I have to say I'm probably the wealthiest man alive. It would be impossible to list everyone who helped and supported me in my journey of writing and sharing stories and recitations. This is the part of the book where I say thank you.

Thank you from the bottom of my heart to my wife, Michelle, for putting up with me, and to my two daughters, to whom this book is dedicated. Thanks to my brothers George and Gary and my sisters Mary Ann, Elsie, and Ruby, as well as my late sister Eva.

Thanks to my late parents, Hilda and Freeman Ingram, for teaching me to be me. Also much appreciation to good friends Ches Deir, Roger Lockyer, Dennis Best, Steve Best, Amelia Reimer, Dave Anthony, Jennifer Martin, Dave Peach, Mike Slade, Jim Warren, Alex Corbett, and Vince Simone.

And for giving me a platform to share my works, I would also like to thank Linda and Eleanor and the monthly song circle as well as the St. John's Storytelling Festival crowd. As well, special thanks to my partners in crime, Dave Paddon, Dave Penny, Hubert Furey, and Ken Parsons.

And I cannot forget my dear Uncle Mose.

Also thanks to Colin Peddle for the back cover photo, and to Flanker Press. Without you, this wouldn't be possible.

There are hundreds more, and to those who feel as though they may have been forgotten, well, you're not and nor will you ever be. I'm just running out of paper. Thank you!

Harry Ingram was born and raised in Arnold's Cove, Placentia Bay, or as Ray Guy would call it, that far greater bay. Reciting and telling stories has always been a core element of Harry's upbringing. In his younger years he was never shy of telling a joke, story, or recitation at a family function or kitchen party. He has always enjoyed sharing the works of others who have paved the way in this genre, but in recent years he has been putting pen to paper and writing his own material. Harry has grown into an accomplished entertainer on various stages sharing his works alongside Hubert Furey, Dave Paddon, and Dave Penny as the popular group From Stage to Stage, and more recently, with Ken Parsons as part of *The Liar's Bench Show*.